"... with only a
monstrous scorpion for crew."

Alan Burt Akers

# Transit To Scorpio

Illustrated by Tim Kirk

Futura Publications Limited
An Orbit Book

An Orbit Book

First published in Great Britain in 1974
by Futura Publications Limited
Copyright © Daw Books, Inc., 1972

ISBN 0 8600 7802 7
Printed in Great Britain by
C. Nicholls & Company Ltd.
The Philips Park Press
Manchester.

Futura Publications Limited
49 Poland Street
London W1A 2LG

# Table of Contents

# LIST OF ILLUSTRATIONS

# A NOTE ON THE TAPES
# FROM AFRICA

In preparing the strange and remarkable story of Dray Prescot for publication I have become overwhelmed at times with the power and presence of his voice.

I have listened to the tapes Geoffrey Dean gave me, over and over again, until I feel I know the man Dray Prescot as much through his voice as by what he reveals in what he says. At times deep and reflective, at others animated and passionate with the fire of his recollections, his voice carries absolute conviction. I cannot vouch for the truth of his story; but if ever a human voice invited belief, then this one does.

How the tapes from Africa came into my possession is soon told. Geoffrey Dean is a childhood friend, a gray, prim, dedicated man of fixed habits, yet for the sake of old friendship when he called me from Washington I was glad to speak with him. He is a government man with one of these shadowy organizations related to the State Department and he told me three years ago he had had occasion to go to West Africa to supervise fieldwork in connection with a famine emergency. Many brilliant young men and women go out with the Foreign Aid programs, and Geoffrey told me of one, an idealistic youngster, Dan Fraser, who had been working harder than a man should up-country.

Fraser told Geoffrey that one day when the situation was almost impossible with horrific numbers of deaths daily a man staggered out of the African forest. Men were dying everywhere around and there was nothing unusual in that. But this man was completely naked, badly wounded, and he was white.

I met Geoffrey Dean for lunch on a flying visit to Washington. We ate well at an exclusive club. Geoffrey brought the conversation around to his telephone call and went on to say that Fraser, who had almost lost control, was shaken and impressed, profoundly impressed, by this stranger.

The famine was killing people by the thousand, massive epidemics were being staved off by daily miracles, aircraft were encountering near-insuperable difficulties flying in supplies; yet in the middle of this chaos and destruction of human life Dan Fraser, an idealistic but seasoned field-worker, was uplifted and strengthened by the character and personality of Dray Prescot. He had given Prescot food and water and bound up his wounds. Prescot could apparently live on next to nothing, his wounds healed rapidly, and when he realized the famine emergency resolutely refused any special treatment. In return Fraser handed across his cassette tape recorder in order that Prescot might record anything he wished. Prescot had a purpose, Fraser said he could see.

"Dan said he was saved by Prescot. They were miles from anywhere and he'd been alone. The strength, the calmness, the vitality of Dray Prescot was amazing. He was a little above middle height with shoulders that made Dan's eyes pop. His hair was brown, and so were his eyes, and they were level and, according to Dan, oddly dominating. Dan sensed an abrasive honesty, a fearless courage, about him. The man was a dynamo, by Dan's account."

Geoffrey pushed the pile of cassettes over to me across that expensive table with the wine glasses and the silver and fine china and the remains of a first-class meal. Outside that exclusive club Washington, the whole of the United States, seemed as far away, suddenly, as the wilderness of Africa from which these tapes had come.

Dray Prescot told Dan Fraser if he did not hear from him inside three years he could do as he saw fit with the tapes. The possibility that they might see publication gave Dray Prescot a deep inner satisfaction, a sense of purpose that Fraser felt held more significance than this mysterious stranger would reveal.

Fraser was extremly busy with the famine—I gathered more from what Geoffrey did not say that the end of the boy's nervous resources was close—and only the appearance of Dray Prescot had saved an ugly situation from sliding into a disaster that would have had international repercussions. Geoffrey Dean speaks little of his work; but

I believe a great deal of foreign health and happiness is owed directly to him.

"I promised to abide by the conditions laid down by Dan Fraser, who would, in any case, have absolutely refused me permission to take the tapes back to America had he not known I would respect his wishes and the wishes of Dray Prescot."

Geoffrey, I had always thought and saw nothing to make me change my mind, had little imagination. He went on: "That famine was a bad one, Alan. Dan had too much to do. When I arrived, Dray Prescot had gone. We were both hellishly busy. Dan did say that he'd seen Prescot, at night, beneath those African stars, staring up, and he'd felt an unease at the big man's expression."

He touched the cassettes with the tip of his finger.

"So—here they are. You'll know what to do with them."

And so I present in book form a transcript of the tapes from Africa. The story they tell is remarkable. I have edited as little as possible. I believe you will detect from the textual evidence how Dray Prescot swings from the expressions of one age to that of another, freely, without any feeling of anachronism. I have omitted much that he says of the customs and conditions of Kregen; but it is my hope that one day a fuller transcript will be possible.

The last cassette ends abruptly in mid-sentence.

The tapes are being published in the hope that anyone who may be able to shed some light on their extraordinary contents will come forward. Somehow, and I cannot explain this, I believe that is why Dray Prescot told his story in the midst of famine and epidemic. There is more to learn of that strange and enigmatic figure, I am confident.

Fraser is a young man dedicated to helping the less fortunate of the world, and Geoffrey Dean is a civil servant quite devoid of imagination. I cannot believe that either of them would have faked these tapes. They are presented in the conviction that however much lacking in proof they may be, what they tell is a real story that really did happen to Dray Prescot on a world many millions of miles from Earth.

*Alan Burt Akers*

## Chapter One

# The Scorpion calls

Although I have had many names and been called many things by the men and beasts of two worlds, I was born plain Dray Prescot.

My parents died when I was young; but I knew them both and loved them deeply. There was no mystery about my birth and I would consider it shameful now to wish that my real father had been a prince, my real mother a princess.

I was born in a small house in the middle of a row of identically similar houses, an only child, and a loved one. Now I find myself often wondering what my parents would make of my strange life and how they would greet with delight or that delicious family mockery my walking with kings and my dealing as an equal with emperors and dictators, and all the palaces and temples and fantastic settings of distant Kregen, that have fashioned me into the man I am today.

My life has been long, incredibly long by any standards, and yet I know I merely stand at the threshold of the many possibilities the future holds. Always, for as long as I can remember, ill-defined dreams and grand and nebulous ambitions enclosed me in a fervent belief that life itself held the answers to everything, and that to understand life was to understand the universe.

Even as a child I would fall into a strange kind of daze in which I would sit back and stare upward sightlessly, my mind blank, receptive of a warm white light that pulsed everywhere. I cannot now say what thoughts passed through my brain for I do not believe I thought at all during those times. If this was the meditation or contemplation so ardently sought by Eastern religions then I had stumbled on secrets far beyond my comprehension.

What is still vividly in my mind of my young days is my mother's apparently continuous letting-out of my clothes as I grew. She would bring out her sewing basket and select a needle and look at me with such an expression of loving helplessness as I stood there, my shirt once more torn across my shoulders. "You'll soon not be able to go through a door, Dray, with those shoulders," she would scold, and then my father would come in, laughing perhaps over my wriggling discomfiture, although we had, as a family, precious little to laugh at in those days.

The sea which boomed and thundered whitely at the mouth of the river had always conveyed to me a siren song; but my father, who carried his certificate of exemption with him day and night, set his face against my going to sea. As the gulls wheeled and called across the marshes and swooped about the old church tower, I would lie on the grass and ponder my future. Had anyone then told me of Kregen beneath Antares and of the marvels and mysteries of that wild and savage world I would have run as though from a leper or a madman.

The natural aversion my father held to the sea was founded on deep suspicion of the morality and system of those responsible for manning the ships. He had all his life lived with horses as his chief interest, capable of dealing with all aspects of their care and training, and when I was born in 1775 he was earning our living by horse-doctoring. During the time I spent with the Clansmen of Felschraung on Kregen long after my father's death I felt myself nearer to him than ever before.

Our spotless kitchen was always crammed with greenish bottles of mysterious mixtures, and the smell of liniments and oils struggled with those of cabbage and freshly-baked bread. There was always weighty talk of the staggers, glanders, pinkeye and strangles. I suppose, speaking logically, I could ride a horse and jump him moderately well before I could toddle safely from our kitchen to the front door.

One day an old hag woman with curious eyes and a bent back and dressed in rags stuffed with straw wandered through the street and suddenly it was the craze for our neighbors to have their fortunes told. It was on this day I discovered that my birthday, the Fifth of November, somehow turned me into a Scorpion, and that Mars was my planet of the ascendant. I had no idea of the meanings of these strange words; but the concept of a scorpion intrigued me and possessed me, so that, although I was forced to indulge in the expected fisticuffs with my friends when they dubbed me The Scorpion, I was secretly thrilled and exultant. This even compensated me for not being an Archer, as I longed, or even a Lion, who I conceived would roar more loudly than that Bull of Bashan the schoolmaster loved to imitate. Do not be surprised that I was taught reading and writing, for my mother had set her heart on my being an office clerk or schoolteacher and so raise myself from that sunken mass of the people for whom I have always felt the most profound respect and sympathy.

When I was about twelve a group of sailormen stayed at the inn where my father sometimes helped with the horses, combing them and speaking to them and even finding raggedy lumps of West Indian sugar for them to nibble and slobber from his upturned palm. On this day, though, my father was ill and was carried into the back room of the inn and placed gently on the old settle there. His face dismayed me. He lay there weak and listless and without the strength to sup from the bowl of strong ale the kindly tavern wench brought him. I wandered disconsolate into the yard with its piles of straw and dung and the smells of horses and ale filling the air with an almost solid miasma.

The sailors were laughing and drinking around something in a wicker cage and, immediately intrigued like all small boys, I went across and pushed between the burly bodies.

"How d'ye like that abed with ye at nights, lad?"

"See how it scuttles! Like a foul Sallee Rover!"

They let me look into the wicker basket, quaffing their ale and laughing and talking in their uncouth sailor way that was, alas, to be all too familiar to me in the days to come.

In the basket a strange creature scuttled to and fro, swinging its tail in the air like a weapon, rocking its whole body from side to side with the violence of its movements.

Its scaly back and the two fierce pincers that opened and shut with such malice repelled me.

"What is it?" I asked, all innocently.

"Why, lad. 'Tis a scorpion."

So this was the creature whose name I bore as a nickname!

I felt the hot shame course through me. I had learned that people like me, Scorpios, are supposed to be secretive; but there was no hiding my reaction. The seamen laughed hugely as at a joke and one clapped me on the back.

"He won't get at you, lad! Tom, here, brought him all the way from India."

I wondered why.

I mumbled out some kind of thank you—politeness was a drudgery of social custom my parents had drummed into me—and took myself off.

How these things happen are secrets well kept by heaven, or by the Star Lords. My father tried to smile at me and I told him Mother would be coming soon and some of the neighbors and we would carry him home on a hurdle. I sat by him for a time and then went to beg another quart of ale. When I returned carrying the pewter tankard my heart seemed to stop.

My father was lying half off the settle, his shoulders on the floor and his legs tangled in the blanket that had been tucked around him. He was glaring in mute horror at the thing on the floor before him; yet that horror was contained within an icy mask of self-control. The scorpion crept toward my father with a hideous lurching roll of its obscenely ugly body. I dashed forward as the thing struck. Filled with horror and revulsion I mashed the tankard down on that vile body. It squashed sickeningly.

Then the room was filled with people, the sailors yelling for their pet, the tavern wenches screaming, ostlers, tapboys, drinkers, everyone, shouting and crying.

After my father died my mother did not linger long and I stood beside the twin graves, alone and friendless, for I had no cousins or aunts or uncles I knew of, and I determined to shake off altogether the dust of my country. The sea had always called me; now I would answer that summons.

The life of a sailor toward the close of the eighteenth century was particularly arduous and I can claim no personal credit that I survived. Many others survived. Many did not. Had I cherished any romantic notions about the sea and ships they would have been speedily dispelled.

With a tenacity that is of my nature, whether I will it or not, I fought my way up from the lower deck. I found patrons willing to assist me in acquiring the necessary education so that I might pass my examinations, and incidentally I ought to say that in finding navigation and seamanship subjects over which I seemed to have an instinctive command puts into a proper perspective my eventual arrival on the quarterdeck. It seems now, looking back, that I walked as though in a somnambulistic trance through that period of my life. There was the determination to escape the foulness of the lower deck, the desire to wear the gold lace of a ship's officer, the occasional moments of extreme danger and terror, and as though to balance out emotion the nights of calm when all the heavens blazed overhead.

Study of the stars was required of a navigator and continually I found my eyes drawn to that jagged constellation of Scorpio with its tail upflung arrogantly against the conjunction of the Milky Way and the ecliptic. In these days when men have walked upon the moon and probes are speeding out beyond Jupiter never to return to Earth, it is difficult to recall the wonder and inner apprehension with which men of an older generation regarded the stars.

One star—Antares—seemed to glow down with a force and fire of hypnotic power upon me.

I stared up from many a deck as we crossed with the Trades, or beat about in blockade, or dozed along in the long calm nights in the tropic heat, and always that distant speck of fire leered on me from where it jointed that sinisterly upraised scorpion's tail, threatening me with the same fate that had overtaken my father.

We know now that the binary Alpha Scorpii, Antares, is four hundred light-years away from our sun and that it blazes four thousand times as brightly; all I knew then was that it seemed to exercise some mesmeric power over me.

In the year in which Trafalgar was fought, the same year, I ought to mention, in which I had once again been disappointed of gaining my step, we were caught up in one of the most violent gales I had ever experienced. Our ship,

*Rockingham,* was thrown about with contemptuous ease
by waves that toppled, marbled with foam, to threaten our
instant destruction should they poop us. The counter rose
soaring against the sky and then, as each successive roller
passed away, sank down and down as though it would
never rise. Our topgallants had long since been struck
down; but the wind wrenched our topmasts away into
splintered ruin and slashed into ribbons even the tough
canvas of the storm jib. At any second we would broach
to, and still those enormous waves pounded and battered
us. Somewhere off the lee bow lay the coast of West
Africa, and thither we were driven helplessly before the
fury of the gale.

To say that I despaired of my life would not be true;
for I had as much irrational desire to cling to life as any
man; but this was by now only a ritual act in defiance of a
malignant fate. Life held little of joy for me; my promotion, my dreams, had all faded away and were gone with
the days that had passed. I was weary of going on and on
in a meaningless ritual. If those sullen waves closed over
my head I would struggle and swim until I was exhausted;
but then when I had done everything a man in honor can
do and should do, I would bid farewell to life with much
regret for what I had failed to achieve, but no regret for a
life that was empty to me.

As *Rockingham* lurched and shuddered in that tremendous sea I felt my life had been wasted. I could see no
real sense of fate in keeping my spirit still alive. I had
fought many times, with many weapons, I had struggled
and battled my way through life, roughly, ever quick to
avenge a wrong, contemptuous of opposition; but life itself
had beaten me in the end.

We struck the sand shoals at the mouth of one of those
vast rivers that empty out of the heart of Africa into the
Atlantic and we shivered to pieces instantly. I surfaced in
that raging sea and caught a balk of timber and was swept
resistlessly on and flung half-drowned upon a shore of
coarse yellow-gray sand. I just lay there sodden, aban-
doned, water dribbling from my mouth.

The warriors found me with the first light.

I opened my eyes to a ring of narrow black shanks and
splayed feet. Anklets of feathers and beads indicated instantly that these black men were warriors and not slaves.
I had never touched the Triangular Trade although tempted

many times; but that would not help me now. To these blacks I was not a strange white apparition. As I stood up and looked at them in their feathers and grotesque head-dresses, their shields and spears, I thought at first they would treat me as a white man engaged in the Trade on the Coast and take me to the nearest factory where there would be others of my kind.

They jabbered at me and one thrust a tentative spear tip at my stomach. I spoke boldly, asking them to take me to the other white men; but after only a few moments I realized none understood English, and my pidgin had been learned in the East Indies. By this time in my life I had grown into full stature, a little above middle height and with those broad shoulders that had been the despair of my mother developed with ropes of muscle that had stood me in good stead before in the midst of storm or battle.

They did not overpower me easily. They did not attempt to kill me for they used their spears with the flat or the butt and I assumed they intended to sell me into slavery with the Arabs of the interior, or to cut my carcass up slowly over a stinking village fire, delicate in their torture.

When they had beaten me down I awoke to my senses lashed to a tree in an odiferous village set above the eternal mangrove swamps, those notorious swamps where a single false step would mean a slow and agonizing death as the rank water gradually slopped up over the distended mouth. The village was surrounded by a palisade on which bleached skulls added a grim warning to strangers, where cooking fires smoked and cur dogs whined. I was left alone. I could only surmise my fate.

Slavery has always been abhorrent to me and I found a grim irony that I should be the recipient of racial revenge for a crime I had not committed. Again the feeling of destiny urging me on overwhelmed me. If I was to die, then I would fight every last step of the way for no other reason than that I was a man.

The bonds around my wrists cut cruelly and yet, as the day wore on in heat and stench and stifling dampness, by continual rubbing and twisting that left my wrists raw some slack became evident. During the afternoon two other survivors of the wreck of *Rockingham* were dragged into the village. One was the bosun, a large surly individual with reddish hair and beard who had evidently put up a fight, for his red hair was caked with dried blood. The other was the purser, still fat and greasy, a man whom no one liked and, as was to be expected, he was now in a pitiable state. They were lashed to stakes on each side of me.

With flies buzzing around us for company we hung and rotted until at blessed last the sun fell. Fresh hordes of insects then took up the task of sucking our blood. I will not dwell on what happened to my two unfortunate companions, hung one on each side of me on their trees of suffering; but their awful cries of torment forced me to chafe even more savagely at my bonds.

Looking back, it seems now that the reason I was left until the last came about because the blacks wanted to use the utmost of their diabolical arts on me, caused, no doubt, because twice during the day I had bodily lifted my legs and kicked a too-importunate inquirer into my condition forcefully in the stomach. I understood as my two companions died why our feet had not been pinioned.

By now it was pitch-dark with the red firelight flickering from the crude walls of the huts and the palisade and grinning in jagged reflections from the naked jaws of the skulls atop their stakes. The blacks danced around me, shaking their weapons, shuffling and stamping their feet, darting in to prod with a spear, springing back out of reach of my kicking feet. Any tiredness of a normal kind is soon learned to be lived with in any life at sea. My fatigue was of a deeper kind. But, grim and unyielding, I determined, as my Anglo-Saxon forebears would say, to die well.

Despite the horror of my position I bore these blacks no ill will. They merely acted according to their lights. No doubt they had seen many a miserable coffle of slaves trudging down to the factory to be branded and herded like cattle aboard the waiting scows; perhaps I made a grave mistake, and these very men were members of the local tribes who bought slaves from the blacks and Arabs of the interior to sell at a profit to the traders on the Coast. Either way, it did not concern me. My one concern was to break that last reluctant strand binding my wrists. If I did not break free very soon I would never do so, and would die a mutilated hulk on the stake.

Firelight reflected redly from the eyeballs of the savages and darted pinpricks of blinding light from their spear blades. They closed in, and I saw that this was the moment when they would begin their devilish practices on me. I put out a last desperate effort; my muscles bulged and the blood thundered in my head. The last strand parted. My arms were afire with the agony of returning circulation, and for a long moment I could do nothing but stand there feeling as though I had dipped my arms in a vat of boiling water.

Then I jumped forward, seized the spear from the first astonished warrior, clubbed him and his companion down, let out a shrill shriek followed by a deep roaring bellow as we used to do when boarding, and raced as fast as my legs would allow between the huts. The crude palisade gate could not stop me, and in an instant I had ripped away the line lashing it to the upright, flung it ajar and bounded out into the jungle night.

Where I was going I, of course, had no real idea. Escape impelled me on. The warriors would be after me this very moment, their shock overcome, running like hunting dogs and with their spears held ready for the deadly cast that would bury the blade in my back.

The instinct that drove me on was so deeply-buried in my subconscious that I could barely comprehend why I ran. That I would die was obvious. But that I would struggle and seek every means to prolong life, that, too, given the nature of the man I eventually understood myself to be, is equally obvious.

When one can run along the fore-topgallant yardarm in a gale on a pitch-black night, one could cross the footbridge to hell.

I ran. They followed and yet, I fancied, they did not follow as fast or with as much vigor as they might and the idea occurred that they might be more frightened than I was myself of this jungle night. But follow they would and capture was inevitable. Where lay safety in this predatory jungle aprowl with unknown dangers and festering with poison? Reaching a cleared space where a tree had fallen and dragged down some of its neighbors I clambered up onto the rotting trunk, dislodging some of the residents as I felt a trickle across my feet like grains of sand blowing in the wind. I kicked out. Up I climbed and there, above me, riding clear of the surrounding vegetation, shone the stars of heaven.

The stars glowed above me and as the familiar constellations met my eyes I turned instinctively to seek out one well-known shape that among all the rest had insistently drawn me with hypnotic power I could neither understand nor explain.

There sparkled the arrogant constellation of Scorpio, with Alpha Scorpii, Antares, blinding my eyes. All the other stars of heaven seemed to fade. I was feverish, light-headed, weak, knowing my sure death followed on stalking feet through the jungle. I had thought to use the stars to guide my escape as they had guided me over the trackless seas. I had thought to use the stars to navigate my way back to the beach. What I hoped to do there God knows. I stared at Scorpio malevolently.

"You killed my father!" Sweat stung my eyes. I was half off my head. "And you seek to do the same to me!" I have no real, coherent memory of what followed, for sweat blinded me, and my breathing pained. But I was aware of a shape like a giant scorpion limned in blue fire. I shook my fist at the Scorpion Star. "I hate you, Scorpion! I hate you! If only you were a man like myself. . . ."

I was falling.

Blue fire coruscated all around, there was blue fire in the stars and blue fire in my eyes, in my head, blinding me, dazzling me. The blue changed to a brilliant malignant green. I fell. I fell with the blue and green fires changing and pulsing brilliantly into red as the red fires of Antares reached out to engulf me.

## Chapter Two

# Down the River Aph

I awoke lying flat on my back.

With my eyes closed I could feel warmth on my face and the flutter of a tiny breeze, and beneath me a familiar motion told me I was aboard a boat. This information did not seem at all strange; after all, had I not spent the last eighteen years of my life at sea? I opened my eyes.

The boat was simply a very large leaf. I stared like a man staggering from Copley's taproom in Plymouth stares owlishly on wan daylight. The leaf sped along the center of a wide river whose green water shone splashing and rippling very merrily alongside. On either bank extended a plain of greenish-yellow grass whose limits were lost beneath a horizon shimmering in heat. The sky blazed whitely down on me. I levered myself upon my elbows. I was stark naked. My wrists chafed and the irritation plucked untidily at my memory.

Then I became extremely still and silent, frozen.

The leaf was large, being a good eighteen feet in length, and its curved stalk rose in a graceful arc like an ancient Greek galley's sternpost. I sat silent and rigid in the bows. Where the sternsheets would be in an ordinary Earthly boat crouched a scorpion fully five feet in length.

The monstrous thing was of a reddish hue, and it pulsated as it swayed from side to side on its eight hairy legs. Its eyes were set on stalks, round and scarlet, half-covered by a thin membrane, and they moved up and down, up and down, with a hypnotic power I had to force myself to conquer. Its pincers could have crushed a fair-sized dog. The tip of its sting-armed tail rose high in the air in a mocking blasphemy of the graceful arc of the leaf-stem—and that tip dripping a poisonous green liquid aimed directly at my defenseless body.

Around its mouth clumps of feelers trembled and its mandibles ground together. If that mandibular array once seized on my throat. . . .

That macabre tableau held for what seemed a very long time as my heart beat with a lurching thump very distressing to me. Scorpion! It was no blown-up Earthly scorpion. Within that grotesque body covered by its exoskeleton-like plates of armor a real vertebrate skeleton must exist to support the gross bulk. Those ever-moving eyes were no eyes a scorpion would use. But those pincers, those mandibles—that sting!

Scorpion! I remembered. I remembered the African night, and the firelight and the gleaming spears and the mad flight through the jungle. So how could I be here, floating down a river on a giant boat-shaped leaf with only a monstrous scorpion for crew? Antares—that red star that had blazed down so powerfully upon me as I sought to escape—Antares at which I had hurled my puny mortal hatred, without a single doubt I knew that some uncanny force had drawn me from my own Earth and that Antares, Alpha Scorpii, now shone luridly in the sky above my head.

Even the gravity was different, lighter, freer, and this I saw might give me some slender chance of survival against this fearsome monster.

Scorpions feed by night. By day they skulk beneath logs and rocks. Stealthily I drew back first one leg and then the other, lifting myself slowly onto my haunches. And all the time my eyes were fixed on the weaving eye stalks before me. One chance I had. One fragile chance to leap forward, first to avoid the scything gripping blows of the twin pincers, second to duck the downward darting sting, and then with a heave and a twist to topple the thing overboard.

My empty hands clenched. If only I had a weapon! Anything, a stout root, a broken bottle, an oar loom, even a cutlass—a man who has lived as I have lived knows the meaning of personal weapons, respects them for their meaning to him. However smartly I could break a man's back with my bare hands, or gouge out an enemy's eyes, a mortal human's natural weapons are a poor substitute for the weapons of bronze and steel with which mankind has struggled out from the caves and the jungles. I felt my nakedness then, my soft flesh and brittle bones, my puny human muscles, and I hungered for a weapon. Whatever force had brought me here had not with kindly consideration also provided me with a pistol, or a cutlass, a spear or shield, and I would have suspected weakness had that mysterious force done so.

No thought entered my mind then that I might dive overboard and swim to the river bank. I do not know why this thought did not occur to me and I think, sometimes, that it had to do with my reluctance to abandon my ship, to betray my own trust in myself, and the feeling that no animal should be allowed to conquer me and that if we were to battle then the prize was this simple leaf boat.

I drew a long slow breath and let it out and drew another, filling my lungs. The air was fresh and sweet. My eyes never left the scarlet rounded eyes at the ends of their stalks as they moved up and down, up and down.

"Well, old fellow," I said in a soft and soothing voice, still not moving in any way that could be the signal for the monster to pounce. "It looks as though it's you or me." The eye stalks weaved up and down, up and down. "And believe me, you ugly Devil's Spawn, it is not going to be me."

Still speaking in a low soothing voice, as I had often heard my father speak to his beloved horses, I went on: "I'd like to rip your belly up to that fat backbone you've got in there and spill your tripes into the river. Sink me, but you're a misbegotten lump of offal."

The situation was ludicrous and looking back now I marvel at my own insensitiveness, although I realize that much has happened since and I am not the man I then was, fresh from the inferno of life aboard an eighteenth century sailing ship, and no doubt prey to all the superstitious nonsense plaguing honest sailormen.

And, truth to tell, I talked not only to soothe the beast but also because talking delayed the time when I must act. I could see the sharpness and the jagged serrations of the pincers, the crushing power of the mandibles and the oozing greenish liquid dribbling from the poised sting. The frog believed the scorpion and gave him passage across the river, and the scorpion stung the frog, because, said the scorpion, it was in his nature. "Well, scorpion, it is in my nature not to let anyone or anything best me without a struggle and loathsome though you are to me I allow it is in your nature to kill me, therefore you must allow it in mine to prevent you. And, if necessary, to kill you to protect myself."

The thing swayed gently from side to side on its eight legs, and it pulsated, and its eyes on their stalks weaved up and down, up and down.

With the palms of both hands flat on the greenish membrane of the leaf between the darker green of the veins, I prepared to hurl myself forward and risk that formidable armament and heave the thing overboard. I tensed, holding a breath, then thrust with all the power of corded muscles in thigh and arm. I shot forward.

The scorpion heaved itself up, its tail curling and uncurling, its pincers clashing—then in a single giant leap it flung itself end-over-end out of the boat. I rushed to the gunwale of the leaf and looked over. A splash surrounding an eight-pointed outline with a stinging whip of tail—and then the scorpion vanished.

It was gone.

I let out that held breath. For the first time I noticed that the thing had not exuded any smell. Had it been real? Or could it have been an hallucination brought on by the fantastic unreality of my experiences? Was I still chasing madly through the African jungle, demented and doomed? Was I still lashed to the stake and was my mind winging into a fantasy world to escape from the agony being inflicted on me? People always pinched themselves in this kind of situation; but I had no need of that crude analysis. I knew I was here, on some other world than Earth, beneath the giant red sun of Antares. I knew it, without a doubt.

Shielding my eyes I looked up at the sky. The light streamed down from the sun, tinged with a reddish hue, warming and reassuring. But a new color crept across the horizon turning the yellowish-green grass more green. As I watched with streaming eyes and sparks shooting through my brain another sun rose into the sky, glowing a molten green, suffusing the river and the plain with light.

This green star was the companion to the giant red star that made up the star we called Antares—later I understood that the words "red giant" were a misnomer—and the quality of the light did not discommode me as much as I would have expected. And, too, there were more surprises in store for me in this new world that explained the more Earthly-type of lighting we receive from our own yellow sun shining here. The leaf had ceased its rocking now and my little command had shipped very little water. I scooped up a handful and drank and found it clean and refreshing.

The best thing to be done now was to allow the leaf to carry me down the river. There would be habitations along the river, if there were people in this world, and I found it all too easy to drift with the current and let things happen as they would.

The river wound in wide sweeping reaches. Occasional shoals of sand shone yellow. There seemed to be a complete absence of trees of any stature, although tall reeds and rushes grew in many places along the banks. By dint of much splashing with my hands and with a seaman's instincts to take best advantage of the set of the current, I eventually drove my craft ashore onto a shelving beach. I ran her up well above the water mark. I did not much fancy walking when I had a perfectly adequate boat at my command.

The reeds were of many varieties. I selected a tall straight-stemmed specimen and by much levering and cursing managed to break off a ten-foot length. This would serve as a punt-pole in the shallows. One variety attracted my attention because I accidentally nicked my arm on its leaf. Again I cursed. Swearing is an occupational disease at sea. This reed grew in clumps with straight round stems perhaps an inch or an inch and a half in diameter; but the thing that attracted me was the leaf, which sprouted upright from the top of each stem to a length of perhaps eighteen inches. This leaf was sharp. The width was of the order of six inches, and the shape was—not surprisingly— that of a leaf-bladed spear. I broke off a bundle at a softer node some six or eight feet from the leaf, and I then had a bundle of spears that I wished I had had when my boat's crew had been aboard an hour ago.

The reeds rapidly dried into a tough hardness under the sunshine and the edge of the blade was sharp enough to allow me to hack down more samples.

Taking stock, I looked across the shining surface of the

river. I had a boat. I had weapons. There was abundant water. And by splitting reeds lengthwise I could fashion lines with which to catch the fish that were undoubtedly swarming in the river waiting with open mouths to be taken. If I couldn't fabricate a hook from a sharpened reed or thorn, I would have to construct fish traps. The future, with people or without, appeared giddyingly attractive.

What had there been in life for me back on Earth? The endless drudgery of sea-toil without reward. Hardship inconceivable to the mind of scientifically-pampered twentieth century man. An eventual certainty of death and the dread possibility of maiming, of having an arm or leg taken off by a roundshot of grape or langrage smashing into my face, hideously disfiguring me, unmanning me, tipping out my intestines onto the holystoned decks. Yes—whatever force had brought me here had done me no disfavor.

A flutter of white caught my eye. A dove circled around, fluttering inquisitively nearer, then taking fright and circling away. I smiled. I couldn't remember the last time I had made so unusual a grimace.

Above the dove I saw another shape, more ominous, hawk-like, planing in hunting circles. I could see the second bird very clearly. It was immense, and it glowed and sparkled with a scarlet coat of feathers, golden feathers encircled its throat and eyes, its legs were black and extended, their claws rigidly outstretched. That bird flaunted a glorious spectacle of color and power. Although at the time it would have been impossible for me to have recalled the lines, now I can only leap to those magnificent words of Gerard Manley Hopkins as he reacts with all a man's mind and body to the achievement of, the mastery of, the thing that is so essentially a bird in the air. And more particularly, knowing now what I could not know then, Hopkins' words have a deeper meaning as he calls the windhover "Kingdom of Daylight's Dauphin."

I shouted and waved my arms at the white dove.

It merely circled a little way farther off and if it was aware of that blunt-headed, wing-extended shape above it gave no sign. The deadly hawk shape with its broad wings with their aerodynamic fingertip-like extensions, the wedge-shaped tail, the squat heavily-muscled head cried aloud their own warning. The nature of the hunting bird is to kill its prey; but I could at least warn the dove.

A piece of reed tossed at the dove merely made it swerve gracefully in the air. The eagle or hawk—for that magnificent scarlet and golden bird was of no Earthly species—swooped down. It ignored the dove. It swooped straight for me. Instinctively I flung up my left arm; but my right thrust forward one of my spears. The bird in a great cup-shaped fluttering of its wings and a powerful down-draft effect of its tail, braked in the air above my head, hovered, emitted one single shrill squawk, and then zoomed upward with long massively powerful beats from its broad wings.

In a moment it dwindled to a dot and then vanished in the heat haze. I looked for the dove only to discover that it had also vanished.

A strong feeling came over me that the birds were no ordinary birds. The dove was of the size of Earthly doves; but the raptor was far larger even than an albatross whose shape in the sky above our sails had become familiar to me in many southerly voyages. I thought of Sinbad and his magical ride aboard a bird; but this bird was not large enough to carry a man, of that I was sure.

As I had promised myself I caught my dinner and with some difficulty found enough dry wood. By using a reed bow I made fire by friction, and almost in no time at all I was reclining and eating beautifully-cooked fish. I hate fish. But I was hungry, and so I ate, and the meal compared very favorably with salt pork ten years in the barrel, and weevily biscuits. I did miss the pea soup; but one couldn't have everything.

I listened very carefully and for some considerable time.

With no knowledge of what hostile creatures there might be in the vicinity I judged it advisable to sleep aboard the boat; my patient listening had not revealed the distant thunder of a falls which would bring to a premature end this river journey. For I was now convinced that I had been brought here for a purpose. What that purpose was I did not know and, truth to tell with a full belly and a pile of grasses for a bed, I did not much care.

So I slept through the red and green and golden afternoon of this alien planet.

When I awoke the green tinged crimson light still flowed from the sky, deeper now but the color values of objects still true. After a time I came to ignore the pervading redness of the light and could pick out whites and yellows as though beneath the old familiar sun that had shone on me all my life.

The river wound on. I saw many strange creatures on that uncanny journey. One there was, a thin-legged animal with a globe-like body and a comical face set atop it, for all the world—this or the Earth—like that of Humpty Dumpty. But it walked on eight immensely long and thin legs—and it walked on the water. It skimmed by me, its legs pumping and down in a confusing net-like motion. The thin webs on its feet must each have been three feet across, and there must have been some kind of valvular action to break the suction created as its weight came on each pad in turn. It skittered away from the leaf boat and I laughed—another strange and somewhat painful movement not only of my mouth but also of my abdomen—as it tiptoed over the river surface.

One of the spears made an excellent paddle by which the boat could be steered. Counting days became meaningless. I did not care.

For the first time in many weary years I felt free and relieved of burdens—of care, of fear, of frustration, of all the intangible horrors that beset a man struggling to find his way through a life that has become meaningless to him. If I were to die, either soon or at a more distant date, well—Death had become a companion all too familiar

Drifting thus in a mellow daze down the river, not bothering to count the turn of days, there occurred times of sudden emergency, of stress and of danger, like the occasion when a great barred water snake attempted to clamber with its stunted forelegs aboard the leaf boat.

The battle was short and incredibly ferocious. The reptile hissed and flicked its forked tongue at me and gaped its barn-door jaws open to reveal the long slimy cavity of its throat down which it intended to dispatch me. I balanced on the leaf, which danced and swayed and tipped in the water, and thrust my spears at the water snake's hooded eyes. My first fierce thrusts were fortunate, for the thing let loose a squeal like swollen sheets shrieking through distorted blocks, and flicked its tongue about and threshed those stumpy forelegs. This creature emitted a smell, unlike that scorpion of my first day in this world.

I stabbed and hacked and the thing, shrieking and squealing, slid back into the water. It made off, curving like a series of giant letter S's laterally in the water.

The encounter filled me only with a fuller awareness of my good fortune.

When the first distant roars of the rapids whispered up the river I was ready. Here the banks rose to a height of between eighteen and twenty feet and were footed with black and red rocks against which the water broke and cascaded, spuming. Ahead the whole surface was broken. Standing braced against a thwart constructed from a number of reeds broken to length and thrust between the sides of the leaf which were amply strong enough, and with my body in a bracket of more reeds attached higher up, I was able to lean out and down and thus gain tremendous leverage with the spear-paddle.

That swirling rush through the rapids exhilarated me. The spray lashed at me, water roared and leaped everywhere, the boat spun and was checked by a thrust of the paddle; the black and crimson rocks rushed past in a smother of foam and the lurching, dipping, twisting progress was like Phaëthon riding his chariot upon the high peaks of the Himalayas.

When the boat reached the foot of the rapids and the river stretched ahead once more, placid and smoothly running, I was almost disappointed. But there were more rapids. Where a prudent man would have beached the boat and then made a porterage, I exulted in the combat between myself and the river; the louder the water roared and smashed against the rocks, the louder I shouted defiance.

Having arrived in this world naked and carrying nothing with me I had no tie for my pigtail and water-drenched as my hair was it now hung freely down my back past my shoulder blades. I promised myself that I would have it cut to a slightly shorter length and never again adopt the required queue and its tie. Some of the men aboard ship had had pigtails that reached to their knees. These they kept coiled up most of the time, only letting them down on Sundays or other special occasions. I had put that life behind me now—along with the pigtail.

Gradually from the horizon into which the great river vanished a range of mountains rose, growing higher day by day. I could see snow on their summits, gleaming cold and distant. The weather remained warm and glorious, the nights balmy, and the skies covered with stars whose constellations remained an enigmatic mystery. The river was now over three miles in width, as best I could judge. There had been no falls for a week—that is, seven appearances and disappearances of the sun—but the sound of thunder now reached my ears in a continuous diapason, swelling in volume perceptibly as the current of the river increased in velocity. The width of the river narrowed sharply; in a morning the banks closed in until they were no more than six cables' length apart, and narrowing all the time.

When the river was two cables' wide I paddled furiously across to the nearer bank, almost deafened by the continuous roaring from ahead. There the river vanished between two vertical faces of rock, crimson as blood, streaked with ebony, harsh, and raking half a mile into the air.

I pulled the boat out of the water and considered. By the smooth humped surface of the river I could tell the enormous power concentrated there. The river was now very deep, the water pent between those frowning precipices. The bank was a mere ledge of rock, above which the cliffs rose towering out of my sight. A bush grew there that I recognized, of a deep green with a profusion of brilliant yellow berries the size of cherries; it was a welcome sight. I picked the yellow cherries and ate them—they tasted like a full-bodied port—while I considered.

After a time I took a spear and set off for the falls.

The sight amazed me. By clinging to a rock at the extreme lip I could look over and down that majestic expanse of water as it slid out and over into nothingness and then arched down until far, far below it battered into the ground once again. A solid sheet of spray sleeted from the outward face of the waterfall and obscured what lay beyond. Below, the pool was like a great white lily spreading in widening circles of foam, with the roaring cataract toppling smoothly downward into its eye.

There was no climbing down the rock.

Again I considered. A force had brought me here. Had it brought me merely to stand and marvel at this waterfall? Must there not be something beyond to which I must go? And if I could not climb down the rock—was there no other way of descent? The sheer volume of noise fashioned itself into words: *"You must! You must!"*

## Chapter Three

# Aphrasöe—City of the Savanti

Still munching those delicious cherries whose delights I had found and often savored higher up the river, I went back to my leaf boat. It was hard with the same kind of tough fibrous hardness the reeds had displayed when cut. But also it had a sinuous suppleness about it that stemmed from its leaf-construction. It would twist and squirm through the rapids, as I had found to my satisfaction.

But would it withstand the battering it was bound to sustain? Would I, a mere mortal human, remain alive under such colossal punishment?

To haul the boat back up the river against that smooth powerful current would be an enormous task. I could not stay here. I ate some of the meat left from the last animal I had brought down with a flung spear higher up the river. On both banks vast herds of various kinds of animals, many of them resembling cattle and deer, had roamed and I had pleasantly varied my diet between them and fish and the other vegetables and berries and cherries—but no animals roamed here.

Thoughtfully I took out of the bottom of the leaf the flat stones I had used as ballast to give better stability. As I did this, as I bundled the spears in a lashing of split reed and secured them to the sides, I knew I had made the only decision fate or whatever other forces involved had decreed.

The leaf boat would float upside-down, this I knew. I strapped myself in with split reeds, flat to the bottom, with the ten-feet long pole to hand. The boat rushed down the current. I knew when we took off and sprang out into thin air.

The boat dipped. The air whistled from my lungs. My ears pained. I was aware of a floating sensation. Just when we hit I must have lost consciousness, for the next thing I remembered was of the boat upside-down, pitching and tossing and going in circles, and of myself hanging in my reed strappings above the greenish gloom of foaming water. It hurt to breathe and I wondered how many ribs I had fractured. But I must get out of the whirlpool. There was not even time to feel thankful I was still alive.

Freeing myself was easy enough with a spear-blade. To right the boat took a little more time; but those broad shoulders of mine did the job and I tumbled in and seized a spear-paddle and, with a series of vigorous thrusts, pushed myself from the dangerous vicinity of the foot of the waterfall. In an instant I was floating free and being whirled away down the river once more.

I breathed in deeply. The pain was not severe. Bruises only.

Only a fool or a madman—or one beloved by the gods—would have dared do what I had done. I looked up at the sheer descending wall of water, at the powerful smooth descent and the foaming caldron where the water struck and bounced in a frothing frenzy, and I knew that luck or no luck, mad or not, beloved of the gods or the prey of the Scorpion, I had come through alive what few men could have survived.

Now I could see what lay on the other side of the mountains.

They extended in a chain all around the horizon, gradually diminishing in size as they trended in a circle until directly before me they were a mere purple thread on the horizon. But obstructing the view directly ahead was a— was a—even now it is difficult to adequately convey that first breathtaking sight of Aphrasöe, the City of the Savants.

The rim wall of mountains formed a crater as vast as a crater on the moon and in the exact center the river flowed into a wide-spreading lake. Rising from the center of the lake grew tall reeds. But their reality dwarfs words. They were each of various thicknesses, ranging from newly-growing specimens of a yard in diameter to mature growths of twenty feet across; at intervals up their stems bulbous swellings grew like Chinese lanterns strung on cords. Up and up soared the reeds, and I was reminded of kelp with its bulges growing up underwater.

From the gracefully arching tops of the reeds long filaments descended again, and I was soon to understand the use to which this multiplicity of lines was put.

I have lived a long life and seen the marvelous steel and concrete towers of New York, have ascended the Eiffel Tower and London's Post Office Tower, have explored the cliff hanging palaces of Inner Tibet; but in no other place in no other world have I found a city quite like Aphrasöe.

The very air was scented as my leaf boat bore me on.

From starboard another river wended across the plain pent between the circular crater walls and joined my river in a wide confluence some three miles from the city and the lake. The lake itself I judged to be five miles across, and the height of the vegetable towers—at that time I could only sit and stare upward, baffled.

How could one call those serene vegetable giants reeds? From the clusters of filaments growing from their tops, down past the protuberances swelling from their stems, many of them the size of an Indian bungalow, many the size of a solid Georgian mansion in old England, right down to the massive girth of their trunks which vanished into the water, they were of themselves, independent, isolate, retaining their own essential nature despite anything that might occur around them. The nearer I approached, the bigger they became. Now I had to crane my head back to stare up at them, and could no longer see their tops for the froth of fronds depending. Those fronds were in perpetual motion, swinging in every direction. I wondered at this.

A boat was approaching me up the river.

Naked as I was, all I could do was smooth my drying hair back and lay hold of a spear, and wait.

Like any sailorman I studied the craft approaching with a critical eye. She was a galley. Long silver-bladed oars rose and fell in a rhythm, feathering perfectly together, giving that short sharp chopping stroke that is the Navy way of driving a boat through water. That was needful in a seaway, where there were waves of consequence; within this landlocked water a longer stroke could have been used. I surmised that the rowing arrangements—to use a landsman's phrase—precluded a long stroke and recovery.

The bows were finely molded and high-raked, with much gilding and silver and gold work. She carried no masts. I waited in silence. Now I could hear, above the sounds of the oars and the bubble of water from her stem, shouted commands; the starboard bank backed water, the larboard continued to pull ahead, and the galley swung around smoothly. Another order was followed by the simultaneous lifting of the oars—how often had I given a similar command!—and the galley drifted gently broadside on as I swung down on the current.

From this angle her lines were clearly apparent; long and low as was to be expected, with that high beak and with a high canopied quarterdeck and poop. People thronged her deck. Some of them were waving. I saw white arms and a multitude of colored clothing. There was even music, wafting gently on the breeze.

Had I wanted to escape there was no escape possible.

As I drifted down, a single oar lowered. My boat ran alongside. Still gripping my spear, I leaped out, onto the blade, and then ran lightly up the loom toward the gunwale. It was a stroke oar. I vaulted the rail to land on the quarterdeck. The canopy overhead rustled in the breeze. The deck was as white as any on a King's Ship. The only person visible here was a man wearing a white tunic and duck trousers who advanced toward me with outstretched hand, smiling, eager.

"Dray Prescot! We are glad to welcome you to Aphrasöe."

Numbly I shook hands.

Above the quarterdeck the poop rose in a splendor of gilt and ornamentation. Up there would be the quartermasters at the tiller. I turned to look forward. I could see row after row of bronzed upturned faces, all smiling and laughing at me. Brawny arms stretched to the oars and muscles bunched as a girl—a girl!—nodded and beat lightly on a tambourine. In time with her gentle strokes the oars bit into the water and the galley smoothly gathered way.

"You are surprised, Dray? But of course. Allow me to present myself. I am Maspero." He gestured negligently. "We do not take much pride in titles in Aphrasöe; but I am often called the tutor. But you are thirsty, hungry? How remiss of me—please allow me to offer you some refreshment. If you will follow me—"

He led off to the stern cabin and, dazed, I followed.

That girl, with her corn-colored hair and laughing face, banging time with her tambourine—she had not taken the slightest notice of my nakedness. I followed Maspero and once more that sense of foreordained destiny encompassed me. He had known my name. He spoke English. Was I, then, in truth in the grip of a fevered dream, hanging near to death on a torture stake in the African jungle?

The chafe in my wrists had all gone. There was nothing now to chain me to reality.

A last look back over my shoulder at this amazing galley revealed that our prow now pointed at the city. We moved forward with a steady solid motion very strange to a sailor accustomed to the rolling and pitching of a frigate in the great waves of the ocean. A white dove flew down from the bright sky, circled the galley, and alighted on that upthrusting prow. I stared at the dove. I remembered that it had flown into my view many times since that first occasion; but the gorgeous scarlet and golden raptor had not returned. The people I had seen were now drifting back onto the deck and their clothes blazed brilliantly in the sunshine as they laughed and gossiped like merry folk at a fair.

The man called Maspero nodded, smiling and genial. "We attempt always to respect the mores and behavior of the cultures invited to Aphrasöe. In your case we know that nakedness can cause embarrassment."

"I'm used to it," I said. But I took from him the plain white shirt and duck trousers—although as my fingers closed on the material I realized I had never encountered it before. It was not cotton or linen. Now, of course, that Earthmen have discovered the use of artificial fibers for clothing, the garments or their like could be found in any chain store. But at the time I was a simple seaman used to heavy worsteds, coarse cottons, and the most elementary of scientific marvels could astonish me. Maspero wore a pair of light yellow satiny slippers. Most of my life—until I eased my way through the hawsehole—I had gone barefoot. Even then my square-toed shoes had been graced by cut-steel buckles, for I could not even afford pinchbeck. Gold buckles, of course, were waiting on the taking of a prize of real value.

We walked through the aft cabin with its simple tasteful furniture constructed from some light wood like sandalwood and Maspero motioned me to a seat beneath the stern windows.

Now it was possible to take stock of him. The first and immediately dominating impression was one of vivacity, of aliveness, alertness, and of an abiding sense of completeness that underlay all he did or said. He had very dark curly hair and was clean-shaven. My own thick brown hair was in not too conspicuous a disarray; but my beard was now reaching the silky stage and was not, I venture to think, too displeasing to the eye. Later on, when they were invented, the name torpedo would be given to that style of beard.

Food was brought by a young girl clad in a charming if immodestly brief costume of leaf-green. There was fresh-baked bread in long rolls after the French fashion, and a silver bowl of fruit including, I was pleased to see, some of the yellow port-flavored cherries. I selected one and chewed with satisfaction.

Maspero smiled and all the skin around his eyes crinkled up. "You have found our Kregish palines tasteful? They grow wild all over Kregen wherever the climate is suitable." He looked at me quizzically. "You seem to be in a remarkable state of preservation."

I took another cherry—another paline, as I recognized I would have henceforth to call them. I did not understand quite what he meant by the last part of his sentence.

"You see, Dray, there is much to tell you and much you must learn. However, by successfully reaching Aphrasöe, you have passed the first test."

"Test?"

"Of course."

I could become angry now. I could lash out in fury at being wantonly dragged through dangers. There was a single redeeming feature in Maspero's favor. Speaking slowly, I said: "When you brought me here did you know what I was doing, where I was, what was happening to me?"

He shook his head and I was about to let my anger boil.

"But we did not bring you, in that sense, Dray. Only by the free exercise of your will could you contrive the journey. Once you had done that, however, the voyage down the river was a very real test. As I said, I am surprised you look so well."

"I enjoyed the river," I told him.

His eyebrows rose. "But the monsters—"

"The scorpion—I suppose he was a house pet of yours?
—gave me a fright. But I doubt if he was really real."

"He was."

"Sink me!" I burst out. "Suppose I'd been killed!"

Maspero laughed. My fists clenched despite the gracious
surroundings and the goblet of wine and the food. "Had
there been a chance of you losing your life you would not
have been entered on the river, Dray. The River Aph is
not to be trifled with."

I told Maspero of my circumstances when the red eye
of Antares had fallen on me in the jungle of Africa and he
nodded sympathetically. He began my education there and
then, telling me many things about this planet called
Kregen. Kregen. How the name fires my blood! How
often I have longed to return to that world beneath the
crimson and emerald suns!

From an inlaid cabinet Maspero took a small golden
box, much engraved, and from this box he lifted a
transparent tube. Inside the tube nestled a number of
round pills. I had never had much time for doctors; I had
seen too much of their bungling work in the cockpit, and I
steadfastly refused to be bled or leeched.

"We of Aphrasöe are the Savanti, Dray. We are an
old people and we revere what we consider to be the right
ways of wisdom and truth, tempered with kindness and
compassion. But we know we are not infallible. It may be
you are not the man for us. We have many entrants
seeking admittance; many are called but few are chosen."

He lifted the transparent tube. "On this world of Kregen there are many local languages, as is inevitable on any
world where growth and expansion is taking place. But
there is one language spoken by everyone and this you
must know." He extended the tube. "Open your mouth."

I did as he bid. Do not ask me what I thought, if
perhaps the idea of poison did not cross my mind. I had
been brought here, of my own free will—maybe—but all
this effort, like the provision of the leaf boat, would
scarcely be wasted the moment they had seen me. Or—
might it? Might I not already have failed whatever schemes
they had in mind for me? I swallowed down the pill
Maspero dispensed.

"Now, Dray, when the pill has dissolved and its genetic

constituents habilitate themselves in your brain, you will
have a complete understanding, both written and oral, of
the chief language of Kregen. That tongue is called
Kregish, for clearly it could bear no other name."

To me, a simple sailorman of the late eighteenth century, this was magic. I then knew nothing of the genetic
code, and of DNA and the other nucleic acids, and of
how imprinted with information they can be absorbed into
the brain. I swallowed down the pill and accepted what
new marvels there might lie in store.

As to the business of a world having many languages,
this was natural and anything else would have been a
foolish dream. We on our Earth almost had a common
language which might be spoken and understood from the
farthest western shores of Ireland across to the eastern
frontiers against the Turk. Latin was such a language; but
that had vanished with the rise of nationalism and the
vernacular.

The galley rocked gently beneath us and Maspero
jumped up. "We have docked!" he cried gaily. "Now you
must see Aphrasöe, the City of the Savanti!"

## Chapter Four

# Baptism

Aphrasöe was Paradise.

There seems to me now no other way of describing that city. Many times I wondered if in very truth I was dead and this was Heaven. So many impressions, so many wonderful insights, so much beauty. Downriver wide acres of gardens and orchards, dairy farms and open ranges, provided an abundance of plenty. Everywhere glowed color and brilliance and lightness, and yet there were many cool places of repose and rest and meditation. The people of Aphrasöe were uniformly kind and considerate, laughing and merry, gentle and compassionate, filled with all the noble sentiments so much talked about on our old Earth and so much ignored in everyday life.

Naturally, I looked for the canker in the bud, the dark secret truth of these people that would reveal them to be a sham, a city of hypocrites. I looked for compulsions I suspected and could never find. In all honest sober truth I believe that if Paradise ever existed among mortal men it is to be found in the City of the Savanti, Aphrasöe on the planet Kregen beneath the crimson and emerald suns of Antares.

In all the wonders that each day opened out to me one of the greatest came on that very first day when Maspero led me into the city growing from the lake.

We left the galley and stepped down onto a granite dock festooned with flowers. Many people thronged here, laughing and chattering, and as we passed toward a tall

domed archway they called out happily: "Lahal, Maspero!
Lahal, Dray Prescot!"

And I understood what Lahal meant—a word of greeting, a word of comradeship. And, too, as the language pill
dissolved within me and its genetic components drifted
into place within my brain, I understood that the word
"Llahal"—pronounced in the Welsh way—was a word of
greeting given by strangers, a word of more formal politeness.

Stretching my lips, which are of the forbidding cut of
habitual sternness, into the unfamiliar rictus of a smile, I
lifted my arm and returned the greetings. "Lahal," I said
as I followed Maspero.

The entranceway led into the interior of one of the
enormous trunks. Having left the Earth in the year of
Trafalgar, I was not prepared for the room in which I
now found myself to rise swiftly upward, pressing my feet
against the floor and bending my knees.

Maspero chuckled.

"Swallow a couple of times, Dray."

My ears performed the usual antics as the Eustachian
tubes cleared. It is unnecessary now to describe lifts or
elevators, save to say that to me they were another wonder of the city. During my stay in Aphrasöe I found
myself, against my will as the days passed, continually
searching for that flaw in the gem, that canker in the bud,
that worm in the heart, that I suspected and that I
dreaded to find. Then, I knew that ways of compulsion
existed that I understood and had used. The press gangs
would dump their unsavory human freight at the receiving
ships, and from the slopships they would come aboard,
miserable, seasick, scared, angry. The cat would tame
them and discipline them along with Billy Pitt's Quota
Men. The discipline was open and understood, a stark fact
of life, given the circumstances a necessary evil. Here I
suspected forces that worked in darkness away from the
sight of honest men.

Subsequently I have seen and studied many systems of
control. On Kregen I have encountered disciplines and
methods of enforcing order that make all the notorious
brainwashing indoctrinations of Earth's political empires
seem as the strictures of a gray-headed mistress at a girls'
school.

If any brainwashing system or any other method of

indoctrination and compulsion existed in Aphrasöe I was not then, and never since as my knowledge has expanded, aware of any secret controls.

When the elevator stopped and the door opened by itself I jumped. I knew nothing of selenium cells and solenoids and their application to self-opening doors. It now sounds droll that among the vagaries of my memory I knew that there existed a thing—whether substance, liquid, fluid or what I knew not and nor did anyone else—called *vis electrica,* named by the English physician Gilbert, obtaining his derivation from the Greek word for amber—electron; and that also I knew that Hauksbee had produced sparks. I had heard of the men Volta and Galvani and their work had excited me—and then the thoughts of making a frog's leg twitch abruptly reminded me of that froggy thought I had had on my leaf boat as that damned great scorpion had sat staring at me with his eyes going up and down, up and down, rather like the elevators within the tree trunks.

I stepped out into fresh scented air. All about me stretched the city. The city! Such a sight no man could see and possibly forget. At this height the lake revealed its almost circular shape, cut into by the many tall trunks—I found myself calling them tree trunks; but they were surely of an incredibly more ancient order of vegetable life than trees. From their tops the massed bunches of tendrils drooped. I admit to a shaming thought then, for the appearance of these dangling lines was faintly similar to those of a cat-o'-nine-tails as it lifts in the fist of the bosun's mate at the gratings.

In the railing of the platform before us a gateway led out onto thin air. Maspero started forward confidently. He touched one of a number of colored buttons set in a small desk with, inscribed above it, the name *Aisle South. Ten.* A platform large enough to accommodate four people within an encircling railing flew toward us through the air and notched itself against the opening in the platform on which we stood. It had come swinging up toward us. I noticed a line extending from a cradle in the center of the aerial platform leading aloft—and guessed at once that this line was really a tendril of the great plants. Maspero politely motioned me aboard. I stepped on and felt the resilience as the line took my weight. Maspero jumped on, released the locking device and at once we swung out and

*"Such a sight no man could see and possibly forget."*

down and gained a tremendous acceleration like a child on the downward arc seated in a playground's swing.

We swung through the air, the line arcing under the wind-pressure above us, flying between the tall trunks and their bulbous houses, and as we swung so I saw many other people swinging past in all directions. Maspero had sat down so that his head was below the transparent windshield and he could speak to me. I stood, letting the wind hurtle past my ears and stream my hair out behind me like a mane.

He explained that a central system prevented tangling; it was complicated but they had machines capable of the task. Computers were unknown—except in their most basic ancient forms—to sailing ship officers. The experience of standing on that platform and swinging dizzily through the air was one of the greatest liberating moments of my life. We curved up in a great graceful arc and docked ourselves against another high platform. At perigee we had skimmed the surface of the lake. We transferred to another platform. This time Maspero had to manipulate the translucent vane, rather like a vertical bird's-tail, that trailed away from the line above our heads. He corrected our course so that we passed in a flash another flying platform. I heard a delighted shriek of girlish laughter as we hurtled by.

"They will play their pranks," Maspero sighed. "She well knew I would give way, the minx."

"Isn't it dangerous?" was my foolish question.

We swooped down on our line, swinging grandly toward the lake, and then up and up we climbed dizzily until once again we notched into a platform around a trunk. Here other people were climbing aboard platforms, pushing off to swoop down like playful children. We covered perhaps a mile in this fashion, and all without a single error or tangle. There was a pattern observable in the line of swinging so that right-angle confrontations were obviated. I could have gone on swinging all day. Swingers, the flying platforms were called, and Aphrasöe was often referred to as The Swinging City.

On one high railed platform a party waited for our swinger and one of them, after the greeting: "Lahal, Maspero," and a quiet, polite word to me, said: "Three graints came through Loti's Pass yesterday. Will you be there?"

"Alas, no. I have matters to attend to. But soon—soon—" The party boarded the swinger and then for the first time I heard the words of farewell that came to mean so much to me. "Happy Swinging, Maspero," called his friend.

"Happy Swinging," replied Maspero, with a smile and a wave.

Happy Swinging. How right those words are to express the delight and joy in life in The Swinging City!

Among the many people swinging from place to place I saw youngsters sitting astride a simple bar, holding in one hand the downward-pointing handle of their guiding vane and with the other waving to everyone they passed as they twisted and turned. It looked so free, so fine, so much a part of the air and the wind, this rushing arcing swinging that I yearned to try my skill.

"We have to sort out the tangles they make from time to time," said Maspero. "But although we age but slowly, age we do. We are not immortals."

When we reached our destination Maspero ushered me into his house fashioned from a gigantic bulbous swelling. It must have been five hundred feet from the lake. Up the center went the trunk containing its elevator, and around it extended a ring of rooms with wide windows overlooking the city and the plants and the lake glinting through the traceries of trunks and swingers.

The place was furnished with impeccable taste and luxury. For a man whose ideas of comfort had been formed by moving from the lower deck into the wardroom I gasped. Maspero made me at home very kindly. There was much to be learned. During the days that followed I learned of this planet Kregen, and dimly sensed the mission the Savanti had set themselves. Put into simple terms I could grasp it was their task to civilize this world but coercion could not be used, it must be done by precept and example, and there were very few of them. They recruited—as far as I could understand—from other worlds of which they seemed to know, to my great surprise, and I was a candidate. I wanted no other future.

The Savanti possessed a driving obligation to help all humanity—they still do—but they needed help to fulfill this self-imposed task. Only certain people would be capable and it was hoped I would be one of them. I find it painfully difficult to detail all the wonderful events of my life in Aphrasöe, The Swinging City, the City of the Savanti. I met many delightful people and was absorbed into their life and culture. On excursions I saw the extent of their cut-off little world within that giant crater. Here they were fashioning the instrument that would bring a similar level of happiness and comfort to all the world.

I saw their papermills and watched as the pulp gradually changed through their whirring spinning machinery into smooth velvety paper, beautiful stock, fit to commemorate the loftiest words in the language. But there was a mystery attached to their paper manufacture. I gathered that on certain times during the year they dispatched caravans of paper which would find its way all over Kregen. But the paper was blank, virginal, waiting to be written on. I sensed the secret here; but could not fathom it.

Very soon I was told to prepare for the baptism. I use the English word as the nearest equivalent to the Kregish, intending no blasphemy. Very early we set out, Maspero, four other tutors whom I now knew and liked, and their four candidates. We took a galley which pulled steadily up the other river, not the Aph but the Zelph. The oarsmen laughed and joked as their brawny arms pulled. I had discussed slavery with Maspero and found in him the same deep hatred of that ignoble institution as burned in me. Among the oarsmen I recognized the man who had asked Maspero if he were hunting the graint. I had myself taken my turn at the oars, feeling the muscles across my back slipping into familiar power lines as I pulled. Slavery was one of the institutions of Kregen that the Savanti must needs change if they were to fulfill their mission.

We pulled as far up the River Zelph as we could and then transferred to a longboat pulled by all of us in turn. I had seen no old men or women, no sick or crippled, in Aphrasöe, and everyone took a cheerful hand at the most menial of tasks. The galley turned back, with the girls at the tiller waving until we were out of sight between craggy gray walls. The water rushed past. It was of a deep plum color, quite unlike that of its sister river Aph. The ten of us pulled against the current.

We then went through rapids, portering the boat, and pressed on. Maspero and the other tutors held instruments that revealed themselves to be of potent power. A giant spider-like beast leaped from a rock to bar our way. I stared rigidly at it—and Maspero calmly leveled his weap-

on; a silvery light issued from the muzzle that quietened
the monster until we were past. It clicked its jaws at us, its
great eyes blank and hostile; but it could not move. I do
not think even the science of Earth can yet reproduce that
peaceful victory over brute force.

One of the candidates was a girl, of a clear cast of
feature with long dark hair, not unprepossessing but in no
way a great beauty. We pushed on, passing many horrific
dangers that were quelled by the silvery fire of the tutors.

At last we reached a natural amphitheater in the rock
where the river plunged down in a cataract that was a
miserable imitation of the one over which I had plunged
on the Aph; but which was nevertheless of considerable
size.

Here we entered a cave. This was the first underground
place I had been on Kregen. The light streamed in with its
usual warm pink glow; but it gradually faded as we
advanced and that pinkness was slowly replaced by an
effulgent blueness—a blueness that reminded me vividly of
the blue fires that had limned my impression of the Scorpion as I had stared upward from the African jungle.

We gathered at the brink of what seemed a simple pool
in the rocky floor of the cave. The water stirred gently,
like heating milk, and wisps of vapor arose from its
surface. The solemnness of the occasion impressed me. A
flight of stairs was cut leading down into the pool. Maspero took me to one side, politely allowing the others to
go first.

The candidates, one after the other, removed their
clothes. Then, with uplifted faces and firm tread, we all
walked down the steps into the water. I felt the warmness
enclosing me and a sensation like a warm mouth kissing
me all over, a sensation like a billion tiny needles pricking
my skin, a sensation that penetrated to the inmost fibers of
what I was, myself, unique and isolate. I walked down the
rocky steps until my head sank beneath the surface.

A great body moved in the milky fluid before me.

When I could hold my breath no longer I returned up
the steps. I am a good swimmer—some have said I must
have been spawned from a mermaid (and when he got up
with a black eye and apologized, for I admit of no
reflection upon my father and mother, I had to admit he
meant nothing ill; that in truth what he said could be
proved by the facts of my swimming ability). Now I can

see they were joking; but in my young days jokes and I were rough bedfellows.

I was the last out. I saw the three young men and they seemed to me strong and healthy and fine-looking. The girl—surely she was not the same girl who had walked with us into the pool? For now she was a resplendent creature, firm of body, with bright eyes and laughing face and red lips ripe for the kissing. She saw me and laughed and then her face changed expression and even Maspero said: "By the Great Savant Himself! Dray Prescot—you must be of the chosen!"

I must admit I felt in better health than I could ever remember. My muscles felt toned up and limber; I could have run ten miles, I could have lifted a ton weight, I could have gone without sleep for a week. Maspero laughed again and handed me my clothes and clapped me on the back.

"Welcome, again, Dray Prescot! Lahal and Lahal!" He chuckled, and then, casually, said: "When you have lived for a thousand years you may return here to be baptized again."

## Chapter Five

# Delia of the Blue Mountains

A thousand years!

I stammered in confusion. We were back in Maspero's house. I could not believe it. I only knew I felt as fit and healthy as I ever had. But a thousand years of life!

"We are not immortals, Dray; but we have work to do and that work will not allow us to die off after three score years and ten."

The wonder of that stayed with me for a long time; and then I pushed it away. Life was still lived from one day to the next.

Maspero apologized for the Savant's atavistic attitudes when we went hunting the graint. From time to time huge wild animals would wander through the few passes into the inner world of the crater and because they would damage the crops and kill the people, they must be caught and returned. But the Savanti had once been warlike and fierce like any Kregan of the outer world. They joyed in the dangers of physical combat; but they would not allow of any danger to their quarry. The dangers where they existed were to the Savanti.

So, like a Kregan war party we went forth onto the plains upriver to hunt the graint. I should mention that Kregen, the planet, Kregish, the language, and Kregan, for the inhabitants of Kregen, is pronounced as though there were an acute accent on the letter "e" in the French fashion. I wore hunting leathers. Soft leather cinctured my waist and was drawn up between my legs. On my left arm a stout leather arm guard might prevent slavering jaws from ripping that arm off. My hair was bound back by a leather fillet. There were no feathers in that band, although Maspero, had he wished, could have filled his fillet with feathers—what the Indians called calling coup—and he joyed and delighted in the hunt, and at the same time woefully deplored his savage and primitive behavior.

I carried the sword Maspero had given me. This sword was not designed to kill. The Savanti delighted in meeting the monsters with various weapons; but their chief joy lay in the Savanti sword, a beautifully balanced arm, straight, not a shortsword, not a broadsword and not a rapier; but a subtle combination that I, for one, would not have believed possible had I not seen and wielded one. I felt it to be an extension of my arm. Of course I did not then know how many men I had killed with cutlass, tomahawk or boarding pike. Pistols at sea almost always became wetted or damp and refused to fire; it was not until two years after my translation to Kregen that, on Earth, the Scottish Reverend Alexander Forsyth perfected his percussion caps. I knew how to use a sword and I had used them in action among the smoke of broadsides in the wild plunge to an enemy's deck. I was not one of those fancy university fencers with a foil like a maid's feather duster; but that old Spaniard, Don Hurtado de Oquendo, had taught me well how to use a rapier, and he had been broad-minded enough to allow me the French as well as the Spanish grip and system. I took no pride in the number of men I had spitted as I took no pride in the numbers whose skulls I had cleft through with a cruder Navy cutlass.

We hunted the graint. The beasts somewhat resembled an Earthly bear with eight legs and jaws that extended for over eighteen inches like a crocodile's. Our only chance against them was speed. We would take turns to dart in and parry those wide-sweeping vicious paws armed with razor-sharp claws. We would parry and duck and then cut or thrust and the Savanti sword would inflict a psychic wound that was directly proportional to the power of our blow. When a graint was subdued the poor beast would be carefully tended and taken back over the hills. To accomplish this the Savanti used what was to me then another miracle.

They possessed a small fleet of flying petal-shaped craft powered in a way that I was not to understand for some time. The graint was strapped down and with a plentiful supply of food and water would be flown back over the passes and deposited in a favored place. If he was stubborn enough to retrace his steps then the Savanti could logically accept his decision and once more we would don our hunting leathers and sally forth.

On one such bright day of summer we sallied out ready for a day's sport that would not injure our quarry and would not harm ourselves if we were quick and lithe enough. I had seen a man brought back with a badly slashed side from which the bright blood poured; he was up and about the next day none the worse. But one could be killed at this game, and this the Savanti accepted as a spice to life. They recognized their own weakness in this desire; but they accepted it as a phenomenon of their human character.

We had subdued two graint and I had wandered a little off on my own seeking the spoor of a third. My friends were resting and eating at our little camp. A shadow passed over my head and, looking up, I saw one of the petal-shaped flying boats skimming close. I ducked and it continued on and hit the ground, bounced, lurched, and skidded askew. Thinking that the Savanti taking a monster back would need help, I ran across.

At that moment the graint I hunted bounded from a low hillock and charged the airboat.

Aboard the airboat were three dead men clad in strange coarse garments of some yellow stuff, hooded, and girdled with a scarlet rope with tassels. Their feet were sandaled. There was also a girl, who cried out in terror.

She was blindfolded.

Her hands were bound behind her and she struggled in a silvery tissue gown. Her hair was of the auburn-tinged brown I have always found attractive. I had no time to look further at her for the graint was clearly intent on eating her for his dinner. I shouted, high and hard, and leaped forward.

Somehow, by continuous struggling, the girl had managed to slide the blindfold down from her eyes. As I charged I cast her a single swift glance. Her large brown eyes were terrified; but as soon as she saw me an entirely different expression filled them. She stopped her screaming at once. She shouted something in a fierce excited tone, a word that sounded like: "Jikai!"

I did not understand; but her meaning was plain.

The graint was a large fellow, a good eight feet tall as he reared back on his hind two pairs of legs and pawed at me with the upper two pairs. His long crocodilian snout gaped and the teeth looked extraordinarily hard and sharp.

I might be playing a game; but he was not, and he was hungry, and the soft flesh of the girl represented a nice juicy dinner to him.

I darted in and instantly leaped back so that his responding blow sliced the air where my head had been. I thrust quickly; but he turned and I had to dive forward and roll over as his other paws clapped together in an attempt to imprison my body. I scrambled up and faced him again. He grunted and snuffled, put all his paws to the ground, and charged at me. I skipped aside at the last moment and slashed down as he passed. The blow would, had the Savanti sword not been charged with its miraculous powers, have lopped off his forequarter. As it was the stun lost him the use of that paw. It was erroneous to call his parts quarters, they were eighths; but my father's horse-training died hard. A damned sight harder than this pesky graint. I jumped in again, ducked the gaping fangs, and thrust. This time his other foreleg went out of action. He roared. He swiped at me and I met the blow with a parry; the edge did not cut into him but again that stunning power drained the strength from that limb.

But I had been slow. His fourth upper limb raked down my side and I felt the blood spurting down my flesh. I also felt the pain; but that had to be pushed aside.

"Jikail" shouted the girl again.

A blow had to be landed on his head. I had scorned to use the superior leaping ability the slightly lessened gravity of Kregen afforded my Earthly muscles as unsporting. These beasts were only doing what was in their nature. But now this girl's life was at stake. I had no choice. As the graint charged in again I leaped up, a good ten feet, and slashed him across the eyes and snout. He went down as though a thirty-two pounder had caught him between wind and water. He rolled over and stuck his eight clawed paws in the air. I felt rather sorry for him.

"Jikail" the girl said again, and now I realized that the three times she had used the word had been with a different inflection. It was a Kregish word, I was sure, yet, for some reason, it had not been dissolved into my neural net along with all the other words of Kregish I had acquired.

Now Maspero and our friends ran up. They looked concerned.

"You are unharmed, Dray?"

"Of course. But let us see to the girl—she is bound—"

As we untied her Maspero grumbled away to himself sotto voce. The others of the Savanti looked with as much ill will as that people ever could look at the bodies of the three men clad in the yellow gowns.

"They will try," Maspero said, helping the girl up. "They believe it, and it is true; but they will take such risks."

I stared at the girl. She was a cripple. Her left leg was twisted and bent, and she walked with an effort, gasping at each painful hobble. I stepped forward and took her up in my arms, cradling her against my naked chest.

"I will carry you," I said.

"I cannot thank you, warrior, for I hate anyone who despises me for my crippling. But I can thank you for my life—Hai, Jikai!"

Maspero looked remarkably distressed.

She was remarkably beautiful. Her body was warm and firm in my arms. Her long silky brown hair with that enraging tint of auburn hung down like a smoky waterfall. I could plunge over that waterfall with great joy. Her brown eyes regarded me with gravity. Her lips were soft, yet firm and beautifully molded, and of such a scarlet as must have existed only in the Garden of Eden.

Of her nose I can only say that its pertness demanded from me the utmost exertion not to lean down and kiss it.

I could not dare to dream of kissing those red lips; for I knew that were I to do so I would drown and sink and succumb and I would not answer for what would happen then.

An airboat flew out from the city. It was a pure white, which surprised me, for all the airboats used to carry the animals back through the passes were brown or red or black. Savanti came from the flier and gently took the girl from me.

"Happy Swinging," I said, unthinking.

She looked at me, obviously not understanding.

"Rembered, Jikai," she said.

Remberee, I knew instantly, was Kregish for *au revoir* or *so long,* or *I'll be seeing you.* But Jikai?

I forced my smile and found to my amazement that to smile on her was easy—too easy.

"Am I not to know your name? I am Dray Prescot."

The white clad Savanti were carrying her to the airboat.

Her grave brown eyes regarded me. She hesitated.

"I am Delia—Delia of Delphond—Delia of the Blue Mountains."

I made a leg, as though I were in my admiral's drawing room in Plymouth among his great ladies.

"I shall see you again, Delia of the Blue Mountains."

The airboat was lifting.

"Yes," she said "Yes, Dray Prescot. I think you will."

The airboat soared away to the City of the Savanti.

# Chapter Six

## Testing time in Paradise

Much I was learning about the planet Kregen as it swung beneath its emerald and crimson suns, and this I feel would best be related when occasion arises, for I must speak of many wild and terrible things, and deeds for which to find a name is difficult. I would stand on the balcony of Maspero's house when the twin suns had gone from the sky and stare upward. Kregen has seven moons, the largest almost twice the size of our own, the smallest a hurtling speck of light low over the landscape. Beneath the seven moons of Kregen I brooded long on the girl Delia of the Blue Mountains.

Maspero was continuing to run his long series of tests on me. I had passed the first by successfully arriving at the city; and he still found amusement that I had enjoyed that voyage down the River Aph. I gathered that many had failed to arrive; they had been defeated by the very conditions that had delighted me.

He carried out what I now realize to be a comprehensive analysis of my brain wave patterns. I began to gather the impression that all was not well.

A great deal of my time was spent indulging in the sports of the Savanti. I have spoken of their uniformly powerful physique and their aptitude for all manner of sport. All I can say is that I did not disgrace myself. I could usually manage to find that extra inch, that last spurt, that final explosive thrust that would bring me victory. They were all hollow victories, of course; for until I was accepted as one of the Savanti, and there were other applicants as I well knew, my life would be incomplete.

When I questioned Maspero about Delia—as I now called her to myself without any self-consciousness—he was unusually evasive. I saw her occasionally, for she had been quartered on the other side of the city, and she still hobbled about on her twisted leg. She refused to tell me where she came from, whether by her own design or by express orders of the Savanti I did not know. There was no government that I could determine; a kind of benevolent anarchy prevailed demanding that when a task needed to be done there would always be willing volunteers. Myself I helped gather crops, work in the paper mills, sweep and clean. Whatever chained Delia's confidences was a force I did not as yet know. And Maspero would shake his head when I questioned him.

When I demanded to know why she had not been cured of her crippled leg, which the Savanti could so easily do, he replied to the effect that she was not one who had, like myself, been called.

"Do you mean because she has not taken the journey down the River Aph?"

"No, no, Dray." He spread his hands helplessly. "She is not as far as we can tell one of the people we need to fulfill our destiny. She came here uninvited."

"But you can cure her."

"Maybe."

He would say no more. A chill gripped me. Was this the canker in the bud that I had suspected and then put aside from me as an unworthy thought?

Strangely enough I had never mentioned the glorious scarlet and golden bird to Maspero. Just how the subject came up was trifling; but as soon as I told him that I had seen the raptor he turned with a quick motion to face me, his eyes fierce, his whole body tense. I was surprised.

"The Gdoinye!" He wiped his forehead. "Why you, Dray?" He whispered the words. "My tests indicate that you are not what we expected. You do not scan aright, and my tests refute all that I know, of you and your ways."

"The dove was from the city?"

"Yes. It was necessary."

I was forcibly reminded how little I knew of the Savanti.

Maspero went out, to confer with his associates, I had no doubt. When he returned his expression was graver than at any time I had known him.

"There may be a chance for you yet, Dray. We do not wish to lose you. If we are to fulfill our mission—and you do not yet understand what that is, despite what you have learned, we must have men of your stamp."

We ate our evening meal in a heavy atmosphere as the moons of Kregen spun past overhead in all their different phases. There were five on view tonight. I munched palines and studied Maspero. He remained withdrawn. At last he raised his head.

"The Gdoinye comes from the Star Lords, the Everoinye. Do not ask me of them, Dray, for I cannot tell you."

I did not ask.

I sensed the chill. I knew that in some way unknown to myself I had failed. I felt the first faint onset of regret.

"What will you do?" I asked.

He moved his hand. "No matter that the Star Lords have an interest in you. That has been known before. It is in your brain patterns. Dray—" He did not go on. At last he said: "Are you happy here, Dray?"

"More happy than I have ever been in my life—with perhaps the exception of when I was very young with my mother and father. But I do not think that applies in this situation."

He shook his head. "I am doing all I can, Dray. I want you to become one of the Savanti, to belong to the city, to join us in what we must do, when you understand fully what that is. It is not easy."

"Maspero," I said. "This is Paradise for me."

"Happy Swinging," he said, and went toward his own apartments in his house.

"Maspero," I called after him. "The girl, Delia of the Blue Mountains. Will you make her well?"

But he did not answer. He went out and the door closed softly.

On the following evening I saw the crippled girl at one of the parties that could be found all over the city. Always there were singing and laughing and dancing, formal entertainments, musical contests, poetic seminars, art displays, a whole gamut of real vivid life. Anything the heart desired could be found in the Swinging City Perhaps twenty people circulated in the relaxed atmosphere of this quiet party given by Golda, the flame-haired beauty with the bold eyes and the lush figure, a woman with whom I had spent a number of pleasant evenings. She greeted me bearing a book, a thick tome of many pages and thin paper, and she smiled tilting her cheek for me to kiss that smooth rosy skin.

"You'll love this one, Dray. It was published in Marlimor, a reasonably civilized city some long way off in another of the seven continents and nine islands, and its legends are really most beautiful."

"Thank you, Golda. You are very kind."

She laughed, holding out the book. Her gown of some silvery lamé glistened. I wore my usual simple white shirt and trousers and was barefoot. My hair had been, as I had promised myself aboard the leaf boat, cut to a neat shoulder length and, in honor of Golda's party, I wore a jeweled fillet in my hair, one of the many presents I had received from friends in the city, among the trophies I had won.

"You were telling me about Gah," said Maspero, walking up with a wine goblet for me. He drank from his own.

Again Golda laughed; but this time a different note crept into her deep voice. "Gah is really an offense in men's nostrils, Maspero, my dear. They delight so in their primitiveness."

Gah was one of the seven continents of Kregen, one where slavery was an established institution, where, so the men claimed, a woman's highest ambition was to be chained up and grovel at a man's feet, to be stripped, to be loaded with symbols of servitude. They even had iron bars at the foot of their beds where a woman might be shackled, naked, to shiver all night. The men claimed this made the girls love them.

"That sort of behavior appeals to some men," said Maspero. He was looking at me as he spoke.

"It's really sick," said Golda.

"They claim it is a deep significant truth, this need of a woman to be subjugated by a man, and dates right back to our primitive past when we were cavemen."

I said: "But we no longer tear flesh from our kill and eat it smoking and raw. We no longer believe that the wind brings babies. Thunder and lightning and storm and flood are no longer mysterious gods with malevolent designs on us. Individuals are individuals. The human spirit festers and grows cankerous and corrupt if one individual enslaves another, whatever the sex, whatever specious arguments about sexuality may be instanced."

Golda nodded. Maspero said: "You are right, Dray, where a civilized people is concerned. But, in Gah, the women subscribe also to this barbaric code."

"More fools them," said Golda. And then, quickly: "No—that is not what I really mean. A man and a woman are alike yet different. So very many men are frightened clean through at the thought of a woman. They overreact. They have no conception in Gah of how a woman is—what she is as a person."

Maspero chuckled. "I've always said that women were people as well."

We talked on, about the latest fashions that had, in some mysterious way, reached Aphrasöe from the outside world. The city contained a pitifully few people to lead a planet. Everyone was needed. Maspero, later on, told me that he was now beginning to feel that I would be really the right fiber—as he put it—one of the privileged few who could shoulder the responsibilities of the Savanti. It would be hard, he said. "Don't think the life will be easy; for you will be worked harder than you have ever worked in your life before—" He held up a hand. "Oh, I know of what you have told me of the conditions aboard your seventy-fours. But you will look back to those days and think them paradise compared with what you, as a Savanti, will have to undergo."

"Aphrasöe is Paradise," I said simply, meaning it.

Then Delia of Delphond hobbled across, her face as twisted as her leg at the effort of walking, her gasps loud and separate, a series of explosive blasts of pain.

I frowned.

Frowning was easy, habitual.

"And in Paradise," I asked Maspero, "what of—?"

"I cannot talk about it, Dray, so please do not ask me."

To have spoken at that moment to Delia would have been a mistake.

As the party was breaking up and the guests were calling "Happy Swinging!" to one another and leaping out into space aboard their swingers, I found Delia and, without a word, put my hand beneath her armpit and so helped her along toward the landing platform where Maspero stood talking gaily with Golda. Delia, after a single angry wrench, allowed me to assist her. She did not speak and I guessed her contempt for her own condition, and her furious resentment of me chained her tongue.

"Delia and I," I said to Maspero, "are engaged to take a boating trip downriver tomorrow. I notice my old leaf boat is still moored at your jetty."

Golda laughed with her tinkly shiver of amusement. She looked with a very kindly eye on Delia. "Surely you don't have to prove anything, Dray? If only Delia could be—" And then she caught Maspero's eye and stopped and my heart warmed toward Golda. There was much I did not yet understand, not least what was the real mission of the Savanti with all their powers on a savage planet like Kregen.

I kissed Golda on the cheek and bowed quietly to Delia, who looked at me with an expression quite amazing, compounded of bafflement, annoyance, pique and— could that be amused affection? For me, plain Dray Prescot hot from the reeking battlesmoke swathing the bloody quarterdecks of my life on Earth?

That she might not meet me at the jetty was an outcome I was prepared to meet when it came. But she was there, dressed in a plain green tunic and short skirt, with silver slippers—one piteously twisted—on her feet and a reed bag in her hand filled with goodies like a flask of wine and fresh bread and palines.

"Lahal, Dray Prescot."

"Lahal, Delia of the Blue Mountains."

Maspero watched us cast off. I had provided a pair of oars and I pulled with that old familiar rhythm. "I thought you might care to see the vineyards this morning," I said, loudly, for Maspero's benefit. I headed downstream.

"Remberee!" called Maspero.

Delia turned to face him from the sternsheets and, together, we called back: "Remberee, Maspero!"

I suddenly shivered in the warm pink sunshine of Antares.

We did not see the vineyards. I circled back along the extreme edge of the lake, and the green sun, which because of its own orbital movement around the red sun rose and set with an independent cycle, cast a deeper glow upon the waters.

I entered the mouth of the River Zelph.

We had not spoken much. She had told me when I asked that her accident had resulted in a fall from an animal—she called it a zorca and I gathered it was a kind of horse—some two years ago. She had no explanation of how she had come to the City of Savanti. When I mentioned the three men, now dead, in the yellow robes, her brow furrowed in puzzlement. "My father," she said, "moved worlds to find a cure for me."

Waiting until we were far enough up the river to be out of range of prying eyes I pulled in for the bank. Here we ate our lunch—and very good it was, to sit in my old leaf boat under the emerald and crimson suns of Antares with a girl who intrigued me and tugged at me and yet who regarded me as merely a warrior; to quaff rich ruby wine and to eat freshly-baked bread and nibble scented cheese and to chew on the ever-luscious palines.

Upon the bank I threw off my white shirt and trousers and donned my hunting leathers that I had earlier concealed beneath a fold of blanket in the bottom of my craft. The soft leather encircled my waist and was drawn up through my legs and looped, the whole being held in position with a wide black leather belt, its gold buckle a trophy won in the arena. My leather baldric went over my shoulder so that the Savanti sword hung at my left side. On my left arm the strong leather straps were belted up. I had also brought with me a pair of leather Savanti hunting gloves, flexible yet strong, thonging to the wrist, and these I now drew on. The leather Savanti hunting boots would remain in my boat until we were forced to walk; I do not like wearing footwear aboard a boat, even though I had been forced to do so when walking the quarterdeck.

The only item of equipment not belonging to a Savanti hunting accouterment was the dagger. Of course, it was of the city; but it was cold steel; it did not possess that miraculous power of stunning without killing. Many times had I saved my own life, and killed quickly, with a knife or dagger in my left hand—I understood that in the old days such a weapon was called a main gauche—in the melee of boarding or storming. It would serve me again now in what I purposed.

Delia cried out in surprise when she saw me, but instantly recovered her habitual poise. Mockingly, she called out: "And who are you hunting today, Dray Prescot? Surely not me?"

Had I been of a more insensitive character I would have felt a fool, dressed up like an idiot; as it was I was too well aware of what lay ahead to allow petty distractions to deflect me.

"We will go now," I said, and settled in the boat and took up the oars and gave way.

If Delia felt any fears at being alone with a man in a boat she did not show them. I believe she had already sized up some, at least, of the character of the Savanti, and knew that the behavior of the people of Gah, for instance, would not be tolerated in the city. Outside, yes, within the precincts of others' cities, yes, for what they did was for the nonce their business. And, too, in her own Delphond a lazy afternoon's pulling on the river with a man meant exactly no more and no less than what the two involved wished.

When I beached the boat at the foot of the first rapids and helped Delia ashore she turned a questioning face to me.

"You must go with me, Delia."

She jerked her head back as I used her name without the rest; but there was no time then to consider what that automatic flinching meant. Certainly, it had to do with my use of her name, not the path on which we now set out.

I had to carry her. She must have guessed at something of what I intended; and I am quite sure she felt no fear, or, feeling it, would allow me to see.

To look back on that wild and harrowing journey up the River Zelph to the cataract and the pool is to marvel at my own foolhardiness. Here I was carrying the most precious object in two worlds, and walking calmly into dangers that would have sent any man screaming in panic, without the protection of the silvery light weapons of the Savanti. I do not remember—I do not want to remember—the number of times I set Delia hastily down and snatched out my sword and met the furious charge of some enraged monster.

There was continuous effort, and cunning, and brute strength. I hacked down the spider-beasts, and the worm-beasts, and all the beetle-beasts that crept and leaped and writhed upon me. I knew that I would get through. I knew that clearly. Delia through it all remained calm, as though in a trance, hobbling along with painful gasps of effort when she could to free me to fight unimpeded. My sword arm did not tire easily. My left hand, wrist and arm were red and running with blood right to the armpit. That cold steel did not stun.

It killed.

They were clever and ferocious, those guardian monsters.

But I was more clever and more ferocious, not because I was in any way intrinsically better than they; but because I guarded Delia of the Blue Mountains.

We reached the little sandy amphitheater among the rocks and plunged into the cave.

I lifted Delia as the pink glow faded and that uncanny blue luminescence grew, and I laughed—I laughed!

Delia could no longer hobble along, and her lips were tightly compressed to keep back her gasps of pain, so I had to carry her into that milky pool. Wisps of vapor curled from the surface. I strode down the wide flight of steps. The liquid lapped my feet, my legs, my chest. I bent my lips to Delia.

"Take a deep breath and hold it. I will bring you out."

She nodded and her chest swelled against me.

I descended the last few steps and stood with my head beneath that milky liquid that was never simple water and felt once more that lapping mouthlike kissing, that million-fold needle-pricking all over my body. I judged when Delia's breath would be failing, for she could not remain as long underwater as I could, and then walked back up the steps.

All our garments, my sword, my belt, everything, had melted away. Naked we emerged from the pool, as, naked, we ought to have entered it.

Delia craned her head around and looked up into my eyes.

"I feel—" she said. Then: "Put me down, Dray Prescot."

Gently I put Delia of Delphond down on the rocky floor.

Her crippled leg was now rounded, firm, as graceful as any leg that had ever existed in any world of the universe. She radiated a glory. She arched her back and breathed in deeply and pushed her glorious hair up and back from beneath and smiled upon me in a dazzlement of wonder.

"Oh, Dray!" she said.

But I was conscious only of her, of her smile, the luminous depths in her eyes; in all the worlds only the face of Delia of the Blue Mountains existed for me; all the rest vanished in an unimportant haze.

"Delia," I breathed. I trembled uncontrollably.

A voice whispered through the still air.

"Oh, unfortunate is the city! Now must occur that which is ordained—"

Beyond Delia, from the milky pool, a vast body lifted. Liquid ran from smooth skin. Pink flesh showed through the whiteness. The size of the body dwarfed us. Delia gasped and huddled close and I closed both my arms about her and stared up defiantly. And, too, now I could feel a strange sensation within me. If my first dip in the pool of baptism had made a new man of me, then this second baptism had rejuvenated me beyond all reason. If I had felt strong before now I felt ten times as powerful. I bounded with vigor and health and energy, defiant, savage, exultant.

"The cripple is cured!" I shouted.

"Begone, Dray Prescot!" The voice from that vast body soughed with sorrow. "You would have been acceptable, and sorely do the Savanti need men like yourself! But you have failed! Begone and begone and never Remberee!"

Delia was a naked soft shape in my arms. I bent my head and pressed my lips on hers and she responded with a joyous love that shocked me through and through.

"Begone!"

I felt the blue luminosity crowding close about me. I was slipping away from this world of Kregen. I shouted.

"I will return!"

"If you can," sighed the voice. "If you can!"

## Chapter Seven

# The Star Lords intervene

"Hey! Jock!" a coarse voice shouted. "Here's some poor devil crawled outta the jungle!"

I opened my eyes. I knew where I was. A wooden palisade crowned with skulls. Thatched huts. The smoke from cooking-pot fires. A coffle of black slaves being herded to the beach and the waiting canoes of the Kroomen. Moored in midstream, on a brown and stinking flood, was a brig. The place stank. Oh, yes, I knew where I was.

The harsh sunlight blazed yellow, stinging my eyes.

I do not believe it necessary or even wise to speak of the next few years. I was able to ship out from the slave factory, nauseatingly aboard the slaver brig, and then in some fashion resume my old life. Promotion to post rank still eluded me; but now I did not care. I hungered for Kregen. I bore the Savanti no ill will. I recognized their essential goodness and I acknowledged that I did not understand all the answers to my questions. I failed to comprehend why they had refused to treat Delia—my Delia! Delia of Delphond, Delia of the Blue Mountains— how many nights I stood by the quarterdeck rail and stared up at the stars and ever and ever my eyes sought that red star that was Antares, and there, I knew, lay all of hope or happiness I wanted in all the universe.

I knew what had happened to me. I had been flung out of Paradise.

Paradise. I had found my heaven and had been debarred from entering.

65

After my life of hardship and struggle Aphrasöe was Paradise.

Now that I have lived so long and have visited Earth many times, always, in some strange way it seems, during times of stress or crisis, I can speak more calmly of my feelings then. So that you may better understand the kind of man I am now, speaking into your little recording apparatus, I should say that on Earth I have amassed a considerable fortune over the years in the normal course of business investment. Had I possessed a hundred times that sum in those days when I once more walked the quarterdeck and plunged into the battlesmoke on Earth I would have given it all, over and over, to be returned once more to Kregen of Antares.

When Lloyd's Patriotic Fund voted me a fifty pound sword of honor I grasped the gaudy thing with its gilt and its seed pearls and I longed to feel once again the firm grip of a Savanti sword in my fist.

I do not believe it possible for anyone of Earth to imagine my state of mind as I thought of the crimson and emerald suns of Kregen, of the seven moons glowing in the night sky against those constellations so alien to Earth and yet so familiar to me. The tortured regrets impelled me to a strange step, for I obtained a scorpion and kept the thing in a cage. I would stare at its ugliness for many minutes on end, and hope that some familiar drowsiness would overtake me. The thing was cursed at by the men when we had to clear for action, and as bulkheads and cabin partitions were removed and struck down, I would have my pet scorpion sent down with the rest.

The Peninsular War opened and I was appointed first lieutenant aboard *Roscommon*, a leaky old tub of a seventy-four whose captain was one of the famous mad captains of the Navy List. Clearly, before me lay a career as a lieutenant until my hairs were gray and I was at last discarded on half pay to rot on the beach. Except that—my hair would not turn gray for a thousand years.

We carried out a number of interesting operations, interesting only in that they provided a strong anodyne for the ache in my soul. We took a French eighty gun ship and were thereby cheered. I heard the officers remarking on the astounding ferocity of my conduct during the boarding. I did not care. After the battle, drained of emotion, I stood on the quarterdeck, gripping the rail, and as always my eyes lifted to the heavens. Alpha Scorpii blazed its mocking ruby fires into my eyes.

Was that a hint of blueness limning Antares? Was that a blue shape leering down on me? The shape of a scorpion?

I reached up my arms.

I heard a cry from the quartermaster, and the midshipman of the watch yelled to the master's mate. I ignored them. The blueness grew. It was. It was!

I reached out and felt that blueness expand and take my consciousness into itself and I shouted, loudly and exultantly: "Kregen!" And: "Delia—Delia of Delphond, my Delia of the Blue Mountains! I return, I return!"

I opened my eyes on a sandy beach with the sound of great waves.

Sick despair clogged my mind. Standing up, I looked around upon a vast heaving sea, a sandy beach, a line of bushes inland and beyond that a prairie vast and wide, extending to the farthest horizon.

The gravity—the sun—the suns!—the feel of the air—yes. Yes, this was the world of Kregen beneath Antares. But—but where was the city? Where the River Aph? Where was Aphrasöe. the City of the Savanti, the Swinging City?

My eyes adjusted quickly to the warm pink sunshine; but I could not see what I wanted to see. I hammered a fist into the sand. Where could I be on the surface of an unknown world? Was I in Loh, that continent of mysteries and veils and hidden walled gardens? Or in Gah, that pathetic semblance of a man's sick dreams where women were chained to bedposts? There were Havilfar and Turismond, continents of which I knew nothing—and there were the other continents and the nine islands and all the seas between.

How I cursed my inadequate knowledge of Kregen!

A shadow fleeted between me and that great bloated red sun. I saw a scarlet feathered bird, with golden feathers about its neck and head, its black legs extended with wicked claws wide, its broad wings stiff and stately as it wheeled in hunting circles above me. I stood up and shook my fist at the Gdoinye. It uttered a harsh croak. After a time of surveillance it began to wheel higher and higher with a lazily powerful wingstroke. When it was but a dot in the sky I heard along the beach a sudden shrill chopped-off cry. A woman's cry.

A girl ran toward me along the beach.

It could only be Delia.

With a great shout of joy I ran toward her.

The devil might take me if I cared where in the whole world of Kregen I was if I could have Delia of the Blue Mountains at my side.

A group of riders burst from the dunes beyond Delia. They rode strange beasts, extremely short-coupled with four long narrow legs poising their bodies more hands high than any horse had any right to be. Each had a single curled horn rising from its forehead. The men wore high helmets of blazing gold. They were clad in purplish-colored jerkins studded with brass nails, a color made into vivid bruise-shine by the light. They carried weapons. And they were gaining on Delia far faster than I could reach her.

She, like myself, was completely naked.

The air in my lungs scorched like fire. I bounded in fantastic leaps, my Earthly muscles scorning the pull of gravity. Once before I had let all my Earthly muscle-power leap out in defense of this girl; now my bounds were truly of fantastic distance. Sand sheeted away at each footstep. But the riders gained on Delia, and now I could see they were not men, although possessing two arms and two legs, for their faces were like nothing so much as the big tabby cat's bewhiskered face I remembered from home. Their slit eyes blazed. I shouted, and then saved my breath for running.

Delia flung both arms up as her foot caught in some driftwood discarded on the beach and she fell. I heard her scream: "Dray Prescot!"

A rider leaned one furred arm down and caught her up around the waist, flicked her over to lie facedown across his saddle. I lunged forward like a demented man. I could not lose her after all, not now, not so soon after finding her again!

The lead rider reined up, those enormously long legs of his mount spindling with muscled power. Sand cascaded, his mount slid backward, then, with a snickering shrill, it had regained its balance. But in those few vital moments I had reached a stirrup. I grasped the booted foot and jerked and pulled as though I could tear the thing's leg clean off.

He screamed and something thwacked down on my

shoulders. I glared up. Delia moaned. The rider threw away his crop in fury and drew a long curved sword and lifted it high. I reached up, took his elbow between my fingers, twisted, and heard the bones grind and snap. The thing shrieked again.

Delia's eyes opened; horror clouded them. "Behind you—"

I whirled and ducked and the curved sword sliced air. Now they were all about me. Swords lifted in a net of steel. I reached again for him who e arm I had mangled. He let out a keening shriek and hauled desperately at his mount's reins. The beast reared, throwing me off. Ducking a swiping sword, silently, I leaped again. I was on the thing's haunches, and so short were they that I half hung over nothingness with my left arm clamped around the rider's waist and my right dragging his head back in that arrogant golden helmet. I heard his neck snap and cast him from me. I slid forward into the saddle, seized the reins and kicked my heels into the flanks of the beast. It shivered and snorted and bounded forward.

Then the world spun around in a blaze of sparks and I saw the sand rising up toward me and, for only a fractional moment of time, felt the hardness of the sandy ground smash all along my face.

They must have left me for dead.

When I recovered, sick and groggy, and looked about, the beach was silent and deserted and only the pitiful humped shape of the dead beast, and the sprawled rider beyond, told of the tragedy that had unfolded here.

At the instant of my success, on the point of escape, I had had my mount shot from under me. The weapon still protruded from the poor thing's flank. It was an eight-foot long spear, the head fashioned from bronze and heavy although not particularly sharp. It was an unhandy weapon.

Beneath the rider—I subsequently learned that these feline-like semi-humans were called Fristles—I found his curved scimitar-like sword. Despite his broken elbow he had retained grasp of his sword hilt. When I had flung him from the high saddle he had fallen so that the point of the blade had entered his stomach with the hilt jammed against the ground. That blade had gone clean through his body and the stained point protruded eight inches past his backbone. The blood was blackened and caked and a few flies—for they exist everywhere—rose as I approached.

I turned him over with my foot, freed his hand from the hilt, put a foot on his body and dragged the sword clear. I cleaned it thoroughly with the sand all about me. I was not thinking at all clearly. I did not care to use this creature's clothes, so I cut up the purple leather and fashioned myself a breechclout after the fashion of Savanti hunting leathers; and I cut from his tunic enough to wind about my left arm. His boots fit me well enough. I slung the sword over my shoulder, its scabbard suspended from a leather baldric, and I felt that when I ran across these cat-people again I would kill very many of them before they could once again wrest Delia of Delphond from me.

The sound of hooves would be muffled to a succession of steady thumps in the sand. At the sound I drew the sword and turned to face the rider who approached. The wind blew grains of sand across the hoofprints; there had been no chance of tracking those who had taken Delia.

"Lahal," the rider called when he was fairly up with me. "Lahal, Jikai."

"Lahal," I likewise replied. I had learned what Jikai could mean in the various inflexions put upon the word. It could mean simply "Kill!" It could mean "Warrior" or "A noble feat of arms" or a number of other related concepts, to do with honor and pride and warrior-status and, inevitably, slaying. It had been used in admiration by Delia of the Blue Mountains, as it had been used by her as a command. I studied the stranger, as I said: "Lahal, Jikai."

For, clearly, he was a warrior.

I had made a mistake in custom and usage; for he made a face and pointed to the dead rider and his mount. "Indeed, it is for me to call you Jikai; what have I done that you know of?"

"As to that," I said, "I doubt not that you are a mighty warrior. But I seek a girl these—things—took."

He had an open, frank face, burned brown by the suns of Antares, with light-colored hair bleached by those suns. He carried a steel helmet at his saddle bow, and his mount was of the same strange high-stepping breed as the dead one at my feet. He wore Leathers, russet-brown, tasseled and fringed after the fashion in New England, and he sat his saddle with the alert carriage yet relaxed air I knew bespoke a master rider. I could not say horseman, although no doubt from sheer familiar usage the word crosses my lips from time to time.

"I am Hap Loder, Jiktar of the First Division of the Clan of Felschraung." The last word, as you can hear, was pronounced deeply with a great sound as of clearing the throat. The way Hap Loder said it, made it sound menacing, prideful, arrogant.

"I am Dray Prescot."

"Now that we have made pappattu, I will fight you at once."

Very little would startle me now. Any other time I'd have been pleased to fight him, if he so desired; but at this imperative time I must find Delia. He dismounted.

"You have not told me if you have seen a girl—" I began. His lance flashed before my eyes.

"Uncouth barbarian! Know you not we cannot speak of anything save obi until we have fought and given or taken obi?"

Furious anger flooded me. Pappattu, I understood, meant introduction. The formalities had been observed; but now this idiot would not tell me of Delia until he had fought me! Well—my captured blade flashed. I would not take long over this.

He went back to that tall-legged animal, stuck the slender willowy lance in its boot, came back with two swords. One was long, heavy, straight, a swashbuckling broadsword. The other was short, straight, simple of construction, a stabbing short sword like a gladius. "I have challenged. Which sword, since that is what you have, will you choose?"

I looked him in the eye. Impatient or not to have the thing done, I recognized honor when I met it. This young man, Hap Loder, was offering me a chance of life, and of death for himself. The powerful broadsword, of course, would not stand against my scimitar, except perhaps on sand. I nodded toward the shortsword. He smiled. "It matters not to me," I said. "But make haste." Then, for he was a fine-looking young man and, as I was to discover, Hap Loder was steel-true honest and fearless, I added: "But I think you would do well to choose the short-sword."

"Yes," he said, and took it up by its grip, replacing the

long broadsword in its scabbard strapped to his mount's
saddle. "Should you win I do not mind giving obi; but I
have no wish to die unnecessarily."

On which fine point of logic we fell to.

He was a fine swordsman, yet the very advantages of
the quick and deadly shortsword were lost to him now.
The shortsword is at its best when used with a shield,
packed with room to play in the long ranks of a disci-
plined army, each man relying on his neighbor. Or in the
close and sweaty melee of the press, when the elbow has
room only to move within the compass of the body, does
the shortsword rule. The great broadsword, too, can be
outfought by a wily and nimble opponent, and I think he
had made the better choice. But he could not match the
demon-driven needs that obsessed me.

"Jikai!" he shouted, and lunged.

I made a few quick passes, left his blade short and
faltering, and then, with the old over-underhand loop, sent
his blade flying. My point hovered at his throat. He stared
up, his eyes suddenly wide.

"Now, Hap Loder, tell me, quick! Have you seen a girl
carried off by such carrion as this dead thing?"

"No, Dray Prescot. I speak truth. I have not."

He scrambled up, backing away from my point. He
drew himself up in the position of attention. He put his
palms to his eyes, his ears, his mouth, and then clasped
them over his heart.

"I make obi to you, Dray Prescott. With my eyes I will
see only good of you, with my ears I will hear only good
of you and with my mouth will I speak only good of you.
And my heart is yours to feast upon."

"I don't want your bloody heart," I told him. "I want to
know where Delia of the Blue Mountains is!"

"Had I that knowledge it would be yours."

I stood looking at him, at a loss. He was a young man,
proud and upstanding, and a fine swordsman. If he got
into many fights he'd be taking obi all the time.

He stirred awkwardly and then bent and retrieved his
sword. I watched, alert, but he fingered the weapon and
then walked across to his animal. He spoke to it for a
moment, soothing it, and a pang of remembrance touched
me.

Then he came back leading it by the reins.

"My zorca is yours, Dray Prescot, seeing that you are afoot, which no clansman may be."

A zorca! So this was the type of animal from which Delia had fallen.

"Are you not a clansman? Would you then not have to walk?"

"Yes. But I have made obi to you."

"Hmm." Then the obvious question asserted itself. "Which way lies Aphrasöe, the City of the Savanti?"

He looked blank.

"There is only one city. I have never heard of any other."

This was the answer I had feared to hear. I must be stranded in some remote and forgotten region of Kregen. Then the truth presented itself painfully. It was Aphrasöe that was isolate and hidden; these people were of the planet Kregen, living a natural human life. I thought of the cat-people—or as natural as their customs and environment allowed.

All I could do was go along with Hap Loder and learn all I could from him. I would find Delia, I would! And to find her I must learn, and quickly, damn quickly, everything I could.

I studied the zorca with its twisted single horn. The saddle was richly decorated, but it was functional, comfortable, and the stirrups were long so that there was nothing here of the bent-legged crouch of the Rotten Row jigger up-and-down. One could ride a long way in that saddle. I fancied I would.

Besides the pair of swords and the willowy lance, Hap Loder owned an ax of a peculiar and deadly character, double-bitted, daggered with six inches of flat-bladed steel. Also he had a short compound bow. I looked at his arsenal with amusement; then again at the bow, with respect. He could have shot me down with that long before I could reach him. I cocked an eye at him.

"Show me your skill with the bow, Hap."

He responded willingly. He strung it with a quick practiced jerk, looking up apologetically. "This is a light hunting bow, Dray Prescot. It has no great power. But I joy to show my skill to you, obi-brother."

A piece of driftwood lay in the sand fifty yards off. Hap Loder put four arrows into the wood—*thunk!*

*thunk! thunk! thunk!*—as fast as he could draw back the string, and loose.

I was impressed.

Maybe that was all the weapon he needed, after all.

Also strapped to the saddle in the confined space allowed to so short-coupled an animal were a number of pieces of armor. Most were steel, although some were of bronze, and it looked as though Hap had built up his harness at different times and from different sources. He told me that a Jiktar commanded a thousand men, and my respect for him increased. The Clan of Felschraung was less than ten miles distant. I have for the moment spoken of distances in Earthly terms; when the time is ripe I will tell you more fully of Kregan methods of mensuration and numerology and of time. With two suns and seven moons the later is complex and fascinating.

I had yearned for years to return to Kregen; now I was here and I must not waste time.

"Wait here, Hap," I said. I leaped up to the saddle. The feeling was at once strange and familiar; but altogether exhilarating. It was not the same as swooping down and zooming up in an Aphrasöean swinger; but as I pounded along with the wind in my hair I felt much the same feelings of freedom and exultation. I would find Delia—I would!

I skidded to a halt before Hap Loder and jumped down.

"We will walk together, Hap."

So we started off toward the Clan of Felschraung.

Loder pulled the Fristle spear from the dead zorca. "It is not good to waste a weapon," he said.

"Where do they come from, Hap? Where would they have taken Delia?"

"I do not know. The wise men may answer you. We have but lately come into this area, for we cover many miles in a year. We wander forever on the great plains."

We left the sea far behind us and I realized I had not seen one sail on all that vast expanse.

I learned that there were many clans wandering the prairies of this continent, whose name, according to Hap Loder, was Segesthes, and that between them was continual conflict as one vast conglomeration of people and animals moved from grazing area to grazing area. The city, which was the only city he knew of and which he had

never seen, was called Zenicce. There was in his demeanor
when he spoke of Zenicce not only hatred but a certain
contempt.

Some few miles inland we ran across the hunting party
from which Hap Loder had parted in chase—a chase,
incidentally, he had lost—and I was introduced. The moment we had made pappattu, the necessary preliminary to
the challenge, Hap cried out that he had made obi to me.

On the bronzed faces of the clansmen I saw a dawning
respect. There were a dozen of them, and two looked as
though they would challenge me, anyway, for the custom
was that any man may challenge any other to take obi;
but the others recognized that if I had beaten Hap Loder
I would also beat them. Hap looked down haughtily.
Among the clansmen honor and fierce pride ruled. Weakness would be instantly singled out and uprooted. I was to
learn of the complicated rituals that governed a clansman's life, and of how by a system of duel and election
their leaders were chosen. But at this time I looked about
ready to fight them all if needs be. And, according to their
custom, had I chosen to do so, then Hap would have
fought at my side until either we had been killed or they
had all made obi to me.

That they had all made obi to Hap was in abeyance at
a time of new pappattu; whenever a new challenge was
made to take obi, all old obis died. In effect this would
never work in practice, and the challenge and the giving
and taking of obi would be left to the two contestants.

One of the men, a surly giant, decided. There seems
always such a one in a group, resentful of his defeat at the
hands of him who has taken obi from him, putting it down
to chance or ill luck, and vengefully always on the lookout
to reclaim what he considers is rightfully his. This one was
a deposed Jiktar. He leaped from his zorca, immediately
pappattu was over, and said to me, sneeringly: "I will
fight you at once."

Hap stiffened and then said: "According to custom, so
be it." He drew his own sword. "This sword is in the
service of Dray Prescot. Remember that."

The fellow, one Lart, stood balanced on the balls of his
feet, a steel-headed spear out-thrust. I caught Hap's eye.
He nodded at the spear across the zorca that was ours.

"It is spears, Dray."

"So be it," I answered, and took the spear, and poised it.

As I had known it would be, it was heavy as to blade and light as to haft, ill-balanced, and clumsy. It would throw reasonably well, and no doubt that was its primary function. But if Lart threw his, and I dodged, I would break his neck.

As we circled each other warily I understood that Hap had challenged me with his sword because that was the weapon I had been wearing. This must be another of their customs.

Lart darted in, thrusting and slashing as he came, hoping to bewilder me with his speed and ferocity. I leaped aside nimbly, not letting the spears touch. The same desperate urgency was on me now as had spurred me on when I had fought Hap Loder. I had to find Delia; not prance about at spear-play with a hulking vengeful lout. But I would not wantonly kill him. The Savanti had taught me that, at the least.

But it was not to be. In a quick flurry of the bronze blade I feinted left, swirled right and thrust and there was Lart, a stupid expression on his face, clutching the haft of my spear which had gone clean through his body. Thick blood oozed along the shaft from the wound. When, with a savage jerk, I wrested the spear out blood spouted.

"He should not have challenged me," I said.

"Well," said Hap, clapping me on the shoulder. "One thing is sure. He has gone to the Plains of Mist. He cannot make obi to you now."

The others laughed at the witticism.

I did not. The fool had asked for it; but I had vowed never to kill unless there was no other way. Then I remembered my more binding vows, and I said to them curtly: "If any of you have seen a girl captured by Fristles, or any of their loathsome kind, tell me now, quickly and with truth."

But none had heard or seen anything of Delia.

I took Lart's zorca, as was proper, and I understood that all his property, after the clan leaders had made their judgment, would be mine. Surrounded by clansmen I rode out for the tents of the Clan of Felschraung. Delia seemed enormously remote to me.

## Chapter Eight

# I take obi of the Clansmen
# of Felschraung

I, Dray Prescot of Earth, sat miserably hunched in the skin tent of a man I had killed and felt all the impotent anger and the frustrations and the agony and the hell of total remorse and sorrow.

Delia was dead.

I had been told this by the clan leaders themselves, who had heard from scouting parties who had seen the Fristles set upon by, as they phrased it, "strange beasts riding stranger beasts" and there was no doubt. But there had to be doubt. How could Delia be dead? It was unthinkable, impossible. There must be a mistake. I questioned the scouts myself, impatient of pappattu and of the challenges that sometimes came. All the camp knew that Hap Loder, a Jiktar of a thousand men, had made obi to Dray Prescot, and there were few challenges. I learned the customs and how it was that ten thousand men could live together without a continual round of challenges. On first meeting, obi could be given or taken. Subsequently, it was a matter for jurisdiction of the wise men and the clan leaders, of custom and of necessity, and of elections when a leader died or fell in battle. I was impatient of it all. I searched the camp for the men, and asked my questions easily enough after I had killed the first three and taken obi from the rest, all of them, to the number of twenty-

six. Their stories tallied. Strange beasts riding beasts had
set upon the Fristles and all the party had been slain.

So I, Dray Prescot of Earth, sat in my skin tent surrounded by the trophies my search had brought me, and
brooded long and agonizingly on what had been lost.

Even then, even then I doubted. Surely no man would
be foolish enough to slay such glorious beauty as Delia of
Delphond? But—but it had been beasts who had attacked.
I shuddered. Would they not see beauty in Delia? And
then, came the horrific thought, perhaps if they did it were
better she were dead.

I believe you, who listen to the tapes spinning between
the heads of your recorder, will forgive me if I do not
dwell on my life among the clansmen of Felschraung. I
spent five years with them. I did not age. By challenge, by
election and duel, I rose in the hierarchy, although this
was not of my seeking. It is an amazing and sobering fact
to realize the power of ten thousand men who have made
obi to one man. By the end of the five years every single
one of the clansmen of Felschraung had made obi to me,
either directly as the result of a victory in combat or
through the indirect method of acknowledging me, with
all the ceremony demanded by obi, as being their lord and
master.

It all meant nothing, of course.

Mainly, it was forced upon me by circumstances and
my saving my own skin. I knew why I wanted to live.
Quite apart from my abhorrence of suicide, despite the
dejection into which I can fall, if I surrendered my life
abjectly and Delia of the Blue Mountains still lived and
needed me—how would I acquit myself on the Plain of
Mists then?

Some days of sunshine and rushing winds as we rode
our zorcas across the wide prairies I would think Delia
truly dead. And then on other days as the rains lashed
down and the pack animals and the endless lines of wagons rolled across the plains, sinking axle-deep into the
mud, I would begin to think that perhaps she still lived.
Often I found myself believing she had in some miraculous
way been transported back to Aphrasöe, the City of the
Savants. If so, that was a happening I could understand
and applaud. I had been discharged from Paradise for
helping her, as being unworthy. Perhaps the Savanti had

reconsidered their verdict. Could I look forward once more to seeing the Swinging City?

That I had under my direct command ten thousand of the fiercest fighters I had ever led was an accident.

Their chief weapon was the laminated reflex bow. I, too, learned the knack of sending five shafts out of five into the chunkrah's eye. The chunkrah, as the reference suggests, was the cattle animal, deep-chested, horned, fierce, superb eating roasted. I had need of this expertise with the bow, for more than once or twice when elections had selected the combatants I fought men who wished to take obi from me with bows. I found a primitive pleasure astride zorca or vove in stalking my opponent, clad in hunting leathers like myself, bow to bow, slipping his arrows and sending my own shafts deep into his breast.

The clansmen used an ancient and superbly thought-out system of warfare. While they used their earth-shaking herds of chunkrah to break down enemy palisades or wagon circles, they considered this a waste of good chunkrah-flesh. They fought when the need arose from within the tightly-drawn wagon circle, the laager of the plains. But they took their fiercest joy in the two riding animals, the vove and the zorca. As a clansman I shared with them the two entirely different exhilarations to be found in charging knee to knee in the massive vove phalanxes and in pirouetting superbly on the nimble zorcas as the flashing shafts from our bows seethed into the hostile ranks.

For the first shock of vove combat when the earth shuddered to the pounding of the hooves, the clansmen used the long, heavy, couched lance, banded with iron and steel. Then they would take to their axes, with which they were irresistible. The broadsword was used, and often; but normally only when the ax was smashed or lost from its thong. With my experience of wielding a tomahawk in boarding parties on my own Earth I was able to hold my own. But an ax has a relatively short cutting edge; a striking sword will wound down almost its whole sharpened length. Even from their zorcas and voves, perched in their high saddles, they could not with their axes best me. I found that in the melee of mounted combat when the mighty voves struggled head to head and the swinging room was restricted, an ax could crushingly do more damage, biting down solidly through steel and bronze and

*"The earth shuddered to the pounding of hooves."*

bone. It was a useful weapon then. But as the press increased and the dust rose choking and blinding and stinging in our sweating eyes and clogging in our riding scarves, the short stabbing sword came into its own, and made short work of opponents against whom axes would clog.

The balanced throwing knife was regarded with some favor by certain of the clans of the great plains, and the terchick, as the form in which it was forged was called by the clansmen—I suspected not from its shape but from the sound it made—was swift and accurate. However, it was essentially the woman's weapon, and the fierce tawny-skinned bright-eyed girls of the clans could hurl their terchicks with unerring skill. In the nuptial ceremony the groom would stand for his bride as she sank a quiver-full of terchicks into the stuffed target sacks at his back. Then, laughing, when all her defenses were gone, he would take her up in his arms and place her tenderly upon his vove for their bridal ride.

The voves were eight-legged, large, savage, horned and tufted, shaggy with a russet color glorious beneath the suns of Antares. Their endurance was legendary. Their hearts would pump loyally for day after day in the long chase if necessary, until the animal dropped dead, still struggling on. They carried the main war divisions of the clansmen, fighting with bulk and strength. The zorcas were lighter, fleeter but without the awe-inspiring stamina of the vove.

After five years it became necessary for me to conquer and take over the Clan of Longuelm. Again there was only a marginal joy in it. Hap Loder, who was now my right-hand man, remarked that I could, if I wished, weld the whole of the clansmen of the great plains into a single mighty fighting force.

"Why, Hap?" I said to him.

"Think of the glory!" His face reflected the shining promises he could see. "A force so powerful nothing could stand in its way. And you could do it, Dray."

"And if I did, whom would we fight?"

His face fell. "I had not thought of that."

"Perhaps," I said to him. "Because there would not then be anyone to fight, it might be worth the doing."

He did not really understand me.

Great wealth reckoned in any terms had been amassed

during that five years. I possessed zorcas and voves by the thousand, and chunkrahs by the tens of thousand. I commanded with the rights of life and death the lives of twenty thousand fighting men, and three times as many women and children. The wagons contained chests of jewels, rare silks of Pandahem, spices from Askinard, ivory from the jungles of Chem. A flick of my fingers could bring a dozen of the most beautiful girls one could find to dance for me. Wine, food, music, literature, good talk and the wisdom of the wise men, all were mine without a thought.

But I merely existed through this time, for all I cared about was Delia of the Blue Mountain, and through her for Aphrasöe where all the luxuries and delicacies of the clansmen would taste immeasurably sweeter.

Life, however, was for the living.

If I have given the impression that obi was a mere matter of a challenge, and a relatively brainless combat, then I do the clansmen a disservice. It carried far more ramifications than that. The wise men, for instance, could not in their aged sagacity be expected to be continually leaping up to swing and sword and shoot a bow. The electoral system balanced out in the end to the benefit of the clan, and the clan leader was a fine fighting man, as would be essential given the conditions of life on the great plains of Segesthes.

I knew that I could count on the absolute and fanatical loyalty of every single man of the clans of Felschraung and Longuelm. I had made it my business to weed out men of Lart's type. The first lieutenant of a King's Ship soon learns to handle men. I could find an inverted, ridiculous pride in the fact that my men owed me loyalty without the need of the lash, and if I fancied they also held me in some affection, I would not be a human being had that not pleased me.

These were poor substitutes for what I had lost.

The clansmen kept no slaves.

There was no need for me to do as I would undoubtedly have done, and freed them all with that procedure's consequent tears and confusions and tragedies. Out on the great plains loyalty and affection between man and man and between man and woman would have clogged had slavery obtruded. We rode like the wind, and like the wind were here and gone before oafish mortals could apprehend. Mysticism came easily on the great plains beneath the seven moons of Kregen.

Most obi challenges were fought mounted; only my own flat feet on which I had been standing those first few times had given me an advantage which later I recognized. A clansman lived in the saddle. When a man and maid joined themselves in the simple nuptials recognized by the elders they would ride off together astride their mounts as a natural extension of the lives they had known. They would always contrive to ride off into the red sun's sunset, and not the green sun's. This I understood. Among the many languages of Kregen—and I soon picked up enough of the clansmen's so that I could converse in that tongue as well as Kregish—there were many and various names for the red sun and the green sun and for all the seven moons, and all the phases of the seven moons. Suffice it that if the need arises I will use the most suitable names; for names are important on Kregen, more, if that be possible, than on Earth. With a name a primitive man may conceive he possesses the inner nature of the thing named. Names were not given lightly, and once given were objects of respect. Yes, names are important, and should not be forgotten.

I will speak no more for the moment of the clansmen of Segesthes but pass on to a day of early spring—the Kregan seasons must revolve like our own so that there is a time of planting and a time of growing and a time of harvesting and a time of feasting; but the binary suns make these elementary distinctions gradually change year by year—when I rode out at the head of a hunting party. The men were happy and carefree, for life was good and, as they said, never had they known a greater Warlord, a mightier Vovedeer, a more furious Zorcander, than Dray Prescot.

We had ventured far to the south, leaving that gleaming sea many miles distant—its name was not on record among the clansmen for they were men of the great plains—and we could include in our grazing swing fresh areas opened up to us by the amalgamation with the clan of Longuelm. This had been one reason for my diplomacy of swords.

Even so we had entered areas unknown to the men of Longuelm and this party was as much a scout as a hunt.

Looking back now I can blame myself for bad scouting,

or for bad generalship. But had our point not missed what he should have seen before he died, all that followed would not have occurred and you would not be listening to this tape.

The ground was breaking with the green growing burgeon of spring as we trotted down between two rounded hills whereon trees grew. We always welcomed trees as signs that water and a break from the plains was near. The air smelled as sweet and fresh as it always does in the better parts of Kregen. The twin suns shone, their emerald and crimson fires casting the twin shadows that were now so usual to me.

We bestrode high-spirited zorcas, and a string of fierce, impatiently following voves trailed in the remuda. A few pack animals, calsanys and Kregen asses, mostly, carried our few belongings for camp. Yes, life was good and free and filled with the zest of high living for all those young men who followed me. The image of Delia of the Blue Mountains remained a constant dull ache within me. Yet I was beginning to accept, at last, that I must go on without her.

The shower of arrows and spears felled four of my men, slew my zorca, and pitched me into the dust. I was up in an instant, sword drawn, and a net closed around my head. I could see weirdly-shaped creatures flinging the nets and I hacked and slashed—and then a club smashed against my head and I went down into unconsciousness.

How could I be surprised when I regained consciousness to find that I was naked, apart from a breechclout, and that my hands were lashed together with cords and that I was yoked to what remained of my men?

We were prodded to our feet and commanded to march.

The beasts who had captured us smelled unpleasantly. They were not above four-foot tall, covered in thick hair of a dun color tending to black at the tips, and each had six limbs. The bottom pair were clad in rough sandals, the upper pair wielded the prodding spears and swords and shields, and the middle pair seemed to serve any other function as it became necessary. They wore slashed tunics of some stuff of brilliant emerald color—the color of the green sun of Antares—and their heads, which were lemon shaped with puffy jaws and lolling chops, were crowned with ridiculous flat caps of emerald velvet. They carried their spears as though they knew how to use them.

"Are you all right, Zorcander?" asked one of my men, and the nearest beast growled like a dog in its throat and beat him over the head. He did not cry out. He was a clansman.

"We must stick together, my clansmen," I shouted, and before the beast could strike me I raised my voice and bellowed: "We will come through yet, my friends."

The spear-blade lashed alongside my head and for a space I stumbled along blinded and weak, and dumb.

The camp to which we were brought was resplendent with richly-decorated marquees, and everywhere signs of opulence and luxury indicated clearly that this hunting party believed in making life on the great plains as comfortable as possible. Lines of zorcas tethered together on one side were matched by lines of another riding animal, an eight-legged beast not unlike a vove, except that they were smaller and lighter and without the ferocious aspect of a vove, without the horns and the fangs. Our own captured zorcas had been brought in, I noticed, and tethered with the others. But our captors had not brought in one single vove. Had I been given to empty gestures, I would have smiled.

A man stepped from a tent and stood wide-legged, his hands on his hips, regarding us with a curl to his lips. He was very white-faced, dark-haired, and he wore tight-fitting leathers over all his body. They were of the same brilliant emerald as the garments worn by the things that had caught us.

I decided it would be something to do to snap his neck; something that might lighten the drabness of days.

He turned his face back toward the tent opening. The tent was the most grandiose in all the camp. We stood bedraggled and naked in the dust.

"Ho, my princess!" the man called. "The Ochs have made a capture that may amuse you."

So, I thought to myself, they have princesses hereabouts, do they?

The princess strolled to the entrance to her tent.

Yes, she was beautiful. After all these years, I must admit she was beautiful. One first noticed her hair, like ripe corn with the morning sun shining on it in a field of our own Earth. Her eyes were the cornflower blue of the flowers one might find in that field. These were old and tired clichés before ever they reached Kregen; but I recall her as I first saw her that day long ago as she stood looking down on where we had been flung captive in the dust.

She lifted a white rounded arm that glowed with the warm pink pulse of blood. Her lips were red, red, and soft like a luscious fruit. She wore an emerald green gown that revealed her throat and arms and the lower portion of her legs, and she wore around her neck a string of blazing emeralds that must have ransomed a city. She looked down on us, and her nostrils pinched together as at an offensive smell. Very beautiful and commanding, she looked, on that day so long ago.

I was lifting my face to look at her.

The man walked across and kicked me.

"Turn your eyes to the dirt, rast, when the Princess Natema passes!"

Within my lashings and the yoke I rolled over and still looked up at her although the man had kicked me cruelly hard.

"Does the princess then not desire admiration from a man's eyes?"

The man went mad.

He kicked and kicked. I rolled about; but the bonds interfered. I heard the princess shouting with anger, and heard her say: "Why clean your boots on the rast, Galna? Prod him with a spear and have done. I weary of this hunt."

Well, if I were to die, then this monkey would die with me.

I tripped him and rolled on him and placed my bound wrists on his throat. His face turned purplish. His eyes protruded. I leered at him.

"You kick me, you blagskite, and you die!"

He gargled at me. There was an uproar. The Ochs ran about waving their spears. I surged upright gripping Galna, and my men on the lashings rose with me. I kicked the first Och in the belly and he tumbled away, screeching. A spear flicked past my body. Galna wore a fancy little sword smothered with jewels. I dropped him as though he were a rattler, and as he fell I managed to drag the little jeweled sticker out. The next Och took the small sword through the throat. It broke off as the beast shrieked and struggled and died.

I flung the hilt at the next Och and cut his head open.

I picked up Galna again, my hands and wrists swelling against the lashings, and hurled him full at the princess.

She gave a cry and vanished within her tent.

Then, as it seemed so often when things were becoming interesting, the sky fell in on me.

Neither of us would ever forget my first meeting with the Princess Nafema Cydones of the Noble House of Esztercari of the City of Zenicce.

## Chapter Nine

# Black marble of Zenicce

The most recalcitrant of slaves were sent to labor in the Jet Mines of Zenicce's marble quarries. On the surface the quarries lay open to the twin suns whose topaz and opal fires blazed down on the white marble and lit it with a million hues and tones. Quarrying the white marble was hard unremitting labor; where we were, down in the Jet Mines, the work was a continual torture.

How many people realize, when they admire a fine piece of black marble statuary, a graceful vase or magnificent architrave, that agony and revulsion have gone into its production? Marble that is black is black because of the infusion of bituminous material. Whenever the marble splits, at every blow, it sends forth a fetid, filthy, stinking odor.

We were completely naked, for we wrapped our breechclouts around our mouths and noses to try in some ineffectual way to diminish that charnel house breath that gushed up at us each time our chisels struck into the stone.

Greasy wicks burned and sputtered in black marble bowls and pushed back a little of the darkness of the mines. In this mine there were twenty of us, and the guards had shut down the hewn-log doors upon us. Only when we had cut and hauled up the requisite amount of marble would they feed us, and if we did not produce we would not be fed. For a full seven days we would labor in the Jet Mines, continually sick, desperately attempting to adjust to the smells and the fatigue, and then we would be let out to labor for seven days in the white marble mines of the surface, and then for a further seven days we would be employed on dragging and ferrying the stones along the canals of the city.

My clansmen and I often missed that third period of seven days, and would rotate seven days in the black below and seven days in the white above. I could remember little of my journey here. The city had been large, impressive, cut by canals and rivers and broad avenues, massed with fine buildings and arcades and dripping with green and purple plants growing riotously over every wall. Many strange-looking peoples thronged the streets, half-beast, half-human, and all, so I understood, in inferior positions, little better than slaves and functionaries.

The most recalcitrant of Zenicce's slaves labored in the Jet Mines. My resentment at slavery was so great that, I confess now, I failed to use my reasoning powers, and I fought back, and lashed out, and snatched the whips from the guards and broke them over their heads before a measure of wisdom returned.

When young Loki, a fine clansman from whom I felt honored to receive obi, died in my arms in the foul deliquescence of the Jet Mines, and the vile miasma from the broken walls of marble breathed its poisonous fumes over us as he sprawled there with his sightless eyes unable to be blessed by the twin fires of Antares, I knew I was responsible for his death, that I had been selfish in my hatred. But the guards were clever. They had split my clansmen into three sections, each laboring on a different shift, so that when aloft in the white quarries and escape a mere matter of planning and execution, I could not take that escape route because the rest of my men were not with me, a third of them down in the Jet Mines where no man would leave a friend.

The guards were recruited from a number of races. There were Ochs, and Fristles, and other beast-humans, notably the Rapas, human monsters who might have been the blasphemous spawn of gray vultures and gray men. Very quick with their whips, were the Rapas, quick and finicky and cutting.

Of all the many foolhardy actions I have made in my life what I did, that day in the Jet Mines of Zenicce, must rank as one of the most stupid, for I know it cost me a great deal to make the decision. At the end of our seven days in that filth and stink when we were let out to go aloft to work the white quarries, I secreted myself behind a stinking rock and waited for the new shift. One of my clansmen in the shuffle of passing slaves caught a friend from the newcomers and hurried him out in my place, so that numbers would tally.

When the massive log doors clashed shut on us I stood up in the lamplight.

"Lahal, Rov Kovno," I said.

Rov Kovno looked at me silently. He was a Jiktar of a thousand, a mighty warrior, barrel-bodied, fair-headed and with a squashed broken nose and an arrogant jut to his chin. He was of the clansmen of Longuelm. I thought I had made a mistake, that I had miscalculated. I thought as I stood there in the lamp-splashed darkness with the stink of that infernal black marble choking my nostrils and mouth that he blamed me for our capture. I waited, standing, silently.

Rov Kovno moved forward. He held the hammer and chisel of our trade. He dropped them into the chippings and dirt of the floor. He put both arms out to me.

"Vovedeer!" he said, and his voice choked. "Zorcander!"

One of the men of his gang, not a clansman but just one more of the unfortunates enslaved by the city of Zenicce, looked at me and spat. "He stayed in here after his shift was up!" he said. He could not believe it. "The man is a fool—or mad! Mad!"

"Speak with respect, cramph, or do not speak at all," growled Rov Kovno. He put the palms of his hands to his ears and his eyes and his mouth, and then over his heart. He had no need to speak, and I was pleased, for it meant my plan could go ahead and free me from that worry.

I grasped his hand. "I cannot escape without taking all my clansmen," I told him. "There is a plan. As soon as you make your escape with your men, Ark Atvar will then make his. My shift will go last."

"Does Ark Atvar know of the plan, Dray Prescot?"

"Not yet."

"Then I will remain here, in the Jet Mines, for the next shift to tell him."

I laughed. There, in the Jet Mines of Zenicce, I, a man not given to empty gestures, laughed.

"Not so, Rov Kovno. That is a task laid on your Vovedeer."

He inclined his head. He knew, as did I, the responsibilities of leadership, of the taking of obi.

We all knew that the first escape would be relatively easy, a clean break from the wherries carrying the blocks of marble from the quarries through the canals to whatever building site in the city had need of them. The second escape would be a little more difficult; but it should be done. The third escape would be the most difficult; and that would fall to my shift; I knew my men would not have it any other way.

I had to give Rov Kovno an agreement that I would order Ark Atvar to make the first escape.

The fanatical loyalty of the clansmen of the great plains of Segesthes is legendary.

On the seventh day of that unremitting shift cutting and moving the huge black stones, Rov Kovno begged me to allow him to remain in that hell to pass on the instructions to Ark Atvar. I may take a foolish pride in thinking he would not have thought any the less of me had I succumbed to his earnest pleas. And, truth to tell, the idea of climbing up out of that pit and seeing once more the daylight and smelling the sweet air of Kregen affected me powerfully.

I said to Rov Kovno, rather harshly: "I have taken obi from you, and I know what obligations the taker of obi owes to the giver. Ask me no more."

And he did not ask me any more.

When Rov Kovno whisked an incoming clansman back out to join his shift and make the numbers up I gagged on the stench of the place and almost broke free. But I restrained myself, and was able to speak almost normally as I said: "Lahal, Ark Atvar."

The ensuing scene was almost a repetition of that before.

No time would be wasted. From the week in the white quarries on the surface the slaves would go for their week transporting the blocks. Then Rov Kovno would escape. That week passed as slowly as any week ever has for me—and it was my third consecutive week in the Jet Mines. No one before, I was told, had survived three weeks in that nauseous hell. All that kept me alive and moving was the thought that I had taken obi from these men, and that I owed them their lives and liberty. I confess that the image of Delia of the Blue Mountains faded then, shaming me, to a thin and distant dream, the stuff of fantasy.

When the logs rolled back and the beast-guards prodded the fresh batch of slaves down I looked at the newcomers with a trembling expectancy. From the looks on the faces of my men I knew—they had never expected me to survive, they had not expected ever to see me again.

Now began the fourth consecutive week in the Jet Mines.

By the last day I was very weak. The abominable stench coiled around my head, reached down with vile tendrils into my stomach, caused me a continuous blinding headache, made it impossible for me to keep anything down. My men worked like demons cutting and loading so that my uselessness would not prevent them from receiving our miserable quota of food and drink let down on ropes. The other slaves with us, not clansmen, grumbled; but a rough kind of comradeship had of necessity grown up and we worked together, well enough.

On that last day as the great black blocks swung up in their cradles, gleaming against the lamplight, we waited for our relief. At last the logs rolled back and the fresh shift of slaves began to descend. I saw shaven-headed Gons, and redheaded men from Loh, and some of the half-human, half-beast men driven as slaves; but not a single clansmen was herded down into the pit.

Rov Kovno and his men had escaped!

There could not be any doubt of it.

As we rose up into the marble quarries with the glinting rock cut in gigantic steps all about us, and we saw the tiny dots of slaves and guards working everywhere on the faces, the great mastodon-like beasts hauling cut blocks, the wherries lying in the docks slowly loading as the derricks swung, I began to think life could begin again.

Parties from the other cells of the Jet Mines were joining our band of twenty as we were marched off. There were thousands of slaves employed here. If twenty or so escaped, the overseers would be blamed; but the work would go on. But those twenty men meant more to me than all the other thousands put together.

"By Diproo the Nimble-fingered!" wheezed a weasel-faced runty little man, blinking and squinting. "How the blessed sunlight stings my eyes!"

His name was Nath, a wiry, furtive little townsman with sparse sandy hair and whiskers, with old scars upon his scrawny body, his ribs a cage upon his flat chest. I had marked him out as of use. By his language I guessed him to be a thief of the city, and consequently one of use to me and my clansmen.

In the air above the quarries hung a constant cloud of dust, rock and marble dust, stirred up by continual activity, and this irritated eyes and nostrils, so that we all cut a piece of our breechclouts to wear across our faces, making the garment briefer than ever. Across from the huddle of swaybacked huts enclosed by a marble palisade where we barracked during our period of seven days in the white quarries I saw a band of slave women chipping marble blocks. Their backs gleamed with sweat and the sweat caught and held a patina of marble chips and dust. They too wore simply the slave breechclout. Around their ankles and joining them in coffles stretched heavy iron chains. There was no romance of slavery here, within the marble quarries of Zenicce.

There were more guards in evidence than usual.

One of my men, young Loku, a Hikdar of a hundred, who was poor dead Loki's brother, reported to me. His fierce warrior's face with its sheen of dust-covered sweat looked gray and sunken; but the vicious look in his eyes reassured me.

"The women told me, Dray Prescot," he said. He had taken a risk, talking to the slave women in broad daylight. "There have been two escapes. One from the marble wherries, the other from these very quarries, last night."

"Good," I said.

Nath, the thief, cleared his throat and spat dust.

"Good for them, bad for us. Now the Rapas, for sure, will strike twice as hard."

Loku would have struck Nath for the disrespect he showed a Vovedeer; but I restrained him. I had need of Nath.

"Find out whose turn it is to feed the vosks," I told Loku, "and arrange for one of us to do that unsavory task."

The vosks were almost completely devoid of intelligence, great fat pig-like animals standing some six feet at

the shoulders, with six legs, a smooth oily skin of a
whitish-yellow color, and atrophied tusks; their uses were
to turn waterwheels, to draw burdens, to operate the
lifting cages, and also to furnish remarkably good juicy
steaks and crisp rashers. We, as slaves, saw them only as
work animals. We ate the same slop as the vosks.

The mastodons which did the really heavy work fed
cheaply on a special kind of grass imported from the
island of Strye.

As well as Rapa guards there were many Rapa slaves
working with us, gray vulturine beings with scrawny necks
and beaked faces, whose gray bodies reeked with their
own unpleasant sweat. They were more restless than most
in the quarries that night as the twin suns sank beneath
the marble rim and the first of the seven moons glided
across the sky.

I made Nath tell me what he knew of this city of
Zenicce.

The city contained approximately one million inhabitants, about the same number as the London of my own
time, but in Zenicce there were uncounted numbers of
slaves, hideously suppressed and manipulated. By means of
the delta arms of the River Nicce and artificially constructed canals as well as by extraordinarily broad avenues, the city was partitioned into independent enclaves.
The pride of House rode very high in Zenicce. Either one
belonged to a House or one was nothing. I learned with
an expression I kept as hard as the marble all about us
beneath the glowing spheres of the first three moons of
Kregen that the House color of the Esztercari Family was
the emerald of the green sun of Kregen. So the cramph
Galna whom I had hurled at the Princess Natema was of
her House. I wondered how he would die, shackled to the
horns of a vove and released across the broad plains of
Segesthes? He would not, I fancied, die well—in which as
I discovered later I did him an injustice.

Across the outer compound a Rapa slave was being
beaten by a pair of Rapa guards. They used their whips
with skill and cunning, and the gray vulture-like being
shrieked and jerked in his chains. He had lost, so the
whisper went around, his hammer and chisel, and if the
overseer so willed it, that was a mortal offense. The vosks
in their patient turning of the capstan bars would haul his
broken body to the topmost step of the marble quarries,

and then he would be flung out and down, to crash a bloody heap on the dust and chippings of the floor a thousand feet below.

In the moon-shadowed dimness of the marble walls Loku crept to my side. His face was just as gray and lined; but a fiercer jut to his chin lifted my spirits.

"We feed the vosks for this sennight," he said, his eyes gleaming in the moonlight.

"And?" I asked.

He drew from his breechclout a hammer and chisel. I nodded. It was death to be found with these tools in the barracks, when not working on the marble faces, or down in the Jet Mines. Down there, shut in by the logs for seven days and seven nights, slaves did not wear their chains. Now, back on the surface, we were heavily chained and shackled. "You have done well, Loku," I said. Then, I added: "We shall not forget Loki, we clansmen of Felschraung."

"May Diproo of the fleet feet aid me now!" moaned Nath. His wizened body shrank back. Loku cuffed him idly, sent him keening to a corner of the marble hut.

I did not think that Nath, the thief, would betray us.

We waited that seven days in the white quarries until it was our turn to take the huge marble slabs in their straw balings onto the wherries and transport them into the city. Somewhere in the city, or better yet out on the open plains, my men would be waiting for us. They had not been recaptured. What was done to recaptured slaves was ugly and obvious, given the circumstances.

All that week extra guards were posted, many of them men in the crimson and emerald livery of the city wardens, men supplied by all Houses as a kind of police force. The Rapas made very free with their whips. The Rapa slaves seethed. My men and I were model slaves.

The glint of marble chippings in the air, the eternal tink-tink-tink of the women trimming stones, the heavier thuds of the hammers on chisels all over the quarry faces, the deeper slicing roars as vosk-powered saws bit in clouds of flying chips and dust, all these sounds frayed at our nerves day after day; but we remained quiet and attentive and docile in our chains.

We took turns to feed the vosks, swilling the remnants of our slops into their troughs, pent between priceless marble walls. The places stank almost as much as the Jet

Mines. They would put their pig-like snouts down and grunt and gulp and waves of the nauseating liquid would pulsate out around our legs, filling our noses with the stench. Those whose duty it was, and whom we had relieved of that duty, thought we were mad. Many guards patrolled, on the alert; but few cared to venture too near the vosk pens, as none ventured into the Jet Mines. One shift had refused to send up the stinking black marble, and had simply been shut in there to die. When other slaves had brought the twisted, ghastly bodies out, the guards paraded them through the workings so that none should miss the lesson.

Gradually, on my orders, we cut down the vosk swill.

On the second to last day the vosks were hungry; but we fed them sufficient to quieten the immediate rumblings of their stomachs. On the penultimate day we did not feed them at all, and they were as recalcitrant as an unpunished slave so that, for a time as I labored at the marble, with the sunshine lancing back from the brilliant surface and dazzling my eyes, I feared I had miscalculated. But the vosks are stupid creatures. At the end of the day they grunted and squealed and fairly broke into ungainly waddles on their way back to their pens. We tempted them with morsels of food, sparingly, and so quietened their uproar.

But they received no more food.

On the last day they were surly, puzzled, drawing their loads and turning their wheels with a stupid pugnacity that made me feel heartily sorry for them and what we were being forced to do to them. The slaves, mostly lads and girls, whose task was to prod them along, gave them a wider berth than usual, and stood well out of their way at evening when the twin suns sank in floods of gold and crimson and emerald.

We carried the great slopping vats of swill to the pens and I managed to spill a quantity of the vile stuff near the boots of a Rapa guard, who croaked his guttural obscenities at me, and I stood the flick of his whip in a good cause, for the guards moved away. We poured the slop down outside the marble walls of the pens. The vosks went hungry on the last night—and in the morning when we should have fed them for the last time before punting our loaded wherries from the docks. They squealed and grunted and some, finding hunger a stimulus to a more primitive action, butted their atrophied tusks against the walls of their pens.

That morning the twin suns of Antares rose with a more resplendent brilliance. We ate hugely of the slop the vosks had not seen. Nath was under the eye of Loku. All our chains had been cut through in stealth and with muffled hammers, and now were lapped about us, ready to be cast off. Nath shivered and called on his pagan god of thieves.

We went aboard the wherry for which we would be responsible, clambering about among the gigantic blocks of marble the women had trimmed clean and square, following the slave masons' chalked marks, and I took the greatest chance of all and went swiftly and quietly in that morning radiance to the vosk pens. I threw open all the gates. With a vosk goad I urged the stupid beasts out, and I joyed to see the idiot ugliness of their faces, the pig-like malice in their tiny eyes. They were hungry. They were loose.

The vosks began to roam the quarries, looking for food.

Guards ran yelling angrily, prodding with spears and swords. I saw one Och, his six limbs agitated, attempt to prod a stupid vosk back and rejoiced at his dumbfounded surprise when the usually docile beast turned on him and knocked him end over end with a resounding thump of those two tiny tusks. Had I been inclined, I would have laughed.

I jumped from the jetty onto our wherry and joined the rest of my men, my chains wrapped about me, as the Rapa guards stalked aboard. There would have been ten of them, I knew, for the citizens of Zenicce were naturally touchy about insufficiently guarded slaves in their city. This morning, because for some unfathomable reason the vosks had gone mad and were overrunning the quarries, there were only six guards.

We pushed off and with the long poles punted slowly along the canal between marble banks.

Soon the banks became brick, and then the first of the houses passed. Mere hovels, these, of people without a House, living on the outskirts of the city, free only in name.

I admit now it was a strange sensation to me to be riding water again.

We passed beneath an ornate granite arch over which

passed the morning procession of market vendors and peddlers and housewives and riffraff and thieves, and all that smell and bustle and morning talk and laughter awoke a thrilling in my veins. The sky grew pinker with that pellucid liquid rose-glow of Kregen on a fine morning. The air as we approached nearer the city grew sweeter, and this alone indicates the putrid atmosphere of the mines in which we had sweated and slaved. The canal debouched into a larger channel whose brick walls rose to a height of some ten feet above the water. On each side the blank walls of houses, each joined to the other, frowned down, their roofs at different heights and forms of architecture so that the skyline formed an attractive frieze against the light.

Sentinels in the colors of their Houses were to be seen at vantage points along those walls. Between enclave and enclave on the perimeter of the city lies always an armed truce.

Close now to our destination we swung out of the broad canal which had steadily increased its freight of traffic. There were light swift double-ended craft which, given the niceties of canal navigation, would be almost certainly some form or model of gondola. There were deep-laden barges, like ours, punted by slaves. There were stately pulling barges gay with awnings and silks, the oarsmen sometimes men, as often as not some outlandish creatures decked out in weird finery, all gold or silver lace with cocked hats gay with plumes. I watched all these strange craft with as strange a hunger in my belly, for I had not seen a boat for years, let alone a ship billowing under full canvas to the royals, heeling to the Trades.

Ahead a truly enormous arch towered over the canal. One side of the bridge laid atop the arch was festooned with ocher and purple trappings; the other side gleamed all in emerald green. We turned up a perimeter canal past the bridge, turning toward the green hand, and soon a more open aspect made itself felt in the architecture. We had entered an enclave. From the colors I knew it to be the enclave of the House of Esztercari and a fierce and unholy joy threatened for a moment to sway me from my purpose.

The building site lay to the rear of a stone jetty. We poled in slowly and more slowly toward the jetty, the water pooling and swirling from the wherry's blunt bows.

*"Ahead a truly enormous arch towered over the canal."*

I nodded to two of my men. They slid their poles inboard
and ducked down in the center of the spaces we had left
between the carefully-stacked marble blocks. I heard short
sharp sounds, as of iron on iron.

A Rapa guard swung around from the bows, looking
back, his vulturine face questioning. I, from my position in
the stern, also looked back as though seeking, like the
guard, for the noise astern. I saw another wherry following ours, loaded with marbles, its crew Rapas, its guards
Ochs. It was coming in very fast, due to our loss of way,
and would collide very soon. I did not mind. Now I could
hear the fresh gurgle of water, bright and cheerful and
inspiriting, welling from inside our wherry.

"What's that racket?" demanded the Rapa in his croaking voice.

I lifted my shoulders to indicate I did not know, and
then jumped down from the high stern and went forward,
as though he had called me, trailing my pole. The wherry
was appreciably lower in the water. A Rapa guard in the
waist made as though to stop me. Him, I struck full force
and knocked down and into the marble blocks where two
of my men seized him and silenced him. Two more Rapa
guards had vanished. Water sloshed and gurgled almost to
the gunwale. Another Rapa guard vanished. I saw Loku,
with Nath at his side, loop a coil of chain about the fifth
guard's bird-like ankles in the big boots and drag him
down out of sight. His beginning shriek chopped off short,
as though a bight of chain had snared his windpipe.

The following wherry had avoided us and was poling
past. No one aboard seemed to be taking any notice of
us—and then I saw why. Instantly fury and outrageous
indignant anger spurted up in me.

The Rapa slaves on the second wherry were slaying
their Och guards with their chains, were flinging the small
six-limbed puffy-faced people overboard in bright splashes
of water.

We were now sinking. Within seconds the canal water
slopped inboard. Now the plan was for us to dive and
swim for the bank, covered by the confusion of the
sinking wherry. But guards were rushing from every direction. The Rapa revolt had sparked an instant reaction, so
clumsy, so violent had it been. Our own escape could not
avoid detection now. The Rapas' wherry touched the jetty
and they boiled ashore, shrieking, inflamed, their grisly
chains whirling in their fists.

## Chapter Ten

# "Dray Prescot, you may incline to me!"

The Princess Natema Cydones of the Noble House of Esztercari had come early that morning to the stone masons' jetty of her enclave to select new marble for the walls of a summer palace she was having built on the eastern side of her estate. That she would be taking marble destined for the building of the new water-rates building did not concern her in the slightest. As far as the princess knew there was nothing she might not have if she wanted it.

As I watched in dumb fury those idiotic Rapa slaves destroy the fruits of my planning I did not know, then, that among the knot of brilliantly attired nobles on the jetty stood the Princess Natema impatiently stamping her jeweled foot on the stone, waiting to have the coverings ripped from the marble so that she might choose the exact stones she coveted.

All I saw was the charging mob of Rapas and the sudden wink and flame of weapons in the sunshine and the ugly whirling of the iron chains.

The Rapas were not so stupid, after all. They had successfully smuggled many more of their fellows aboard the wherry. They had been aided in this, without a doubt, by my ruse with the vosks. They were a formidable scarecrow crew in their rags and chains who roared onto

101

the landing. Almost at once brilliant emerald green uniforms were flying through the air and splashing into the waters of the canal.

There was a chance for us, after all. . . .

"Loku!" I cried. "Now! Nath—it is up to you to show the way through the city. We depend on you—if you fail us you know what your fate will be."

"Auee!" he cried, and he grasped his left arm with his right fist, as though it were broken. "By the Great Diproo Himself, I won't fail! I dare not!" And he dived over the side. Those of my men who could not swim, and the clansmen often practiced the art in the lonely tarns of the moorlands far to the north, were equipped with balks of timber. They now all took to the water and began swimming for the far bank. There everything would be up to Nath.

I waited, as a Vovedeer, as a Zorcander, should. A leader of a clan is called that, a leader. When two or more clans are joined together under one leader he is then entitled to take the name of Vovedeer, Zorcander, the derivations of these names being obvious. The taking of obi becomes then that much more of a responsibility. So I waited until all my men were safely away.

They had thrown off their chains; I still gripped a bight of mine between my fists, ready.

The wherry had ceased its last drifting and was now nuzzled bows up against the larboard quarter of the Rapa wherry. The canal here was shallow, and the wherry with its marble freight had sunk until its bottom touched the silt and mud. Now about four feet of marble blocks stood above the water. I crouched on a block between two others, watching.

From the shrieks and screams, the pandemonium and the fierce clash of sword and spear on iron chain I guessed more guardsmen had run up and were engaged in the task, no doubt not entirely unenjoyable to the soldiery, of butchering the last of the slaves. I could take no part in that. My duty lay with my men.

A new timbre arose in the din. Perhaps the slaves were not being dismissed so easily. I chanced a peek around a block and saw the sunshine lying athwart the jetty, with the guards and the Rapa slaves battling in a savage and unholy conflict. Iron chains whirled with reckless and desperate courage make fearsome weapons.

I saw three men bundling a woman into a small low skiff by the jetty wall. Evidently they had been caught by the slaves' first onslaught and were unable to escape. Now the canal was their only chance. The skiff cast off and swung and collided with the first wherry and a flung chain fairly took the head from the man at the oars so that he lolled all dripping and bloody over the side. The woman screamed. The second man seized the oars; but the body cumbered him. The skiff bounced down the side of the wherry. Now a group of slaves seized their chance.

With shrill vulturine shrieks they leaped onto the marble blocks of the wherry, bounded to the stern and leaped down into the skiff. It plunged wildly in the water. The two men, and their dead companion, were tipped overboard without ceremony. Two Rapas seized the oars. Another pair sprawled in the sternsheets, their chains still whirling in reflexive violence. A fifth jumped forward and seized the woman about the waist and pressed her to him, twisting and holding her up so that she could be clearly seen from the jetty.

His intentions were plain.

"Let us go!" he shrilled. "Or the woman dies!"

A confused shouting rose above the battle din.

The woman's screams knifed through the uproar, and unsettled me. I thought of my men, waiting for me. I thought of Delia. I do not know what I thought.

I only know I could not see a woman killed this way, so uselessly. If you ask me if it had been human slaves escaping and using the despised body of an aristocratic woman to shield them, I do not know how I would answer.

Without a sound I jumped from the sunken wherry into the skiff. I tried not to kill. I toppled the two oarsmen overboard. The two men in the bows reared up, their chains chirring with ugly menace.

"Slave—die!" and "Human—perish!" they shouted.

Had they not shouted that, perhaps I would not have fought as I did. But I did fight. My chain blurred through the air and sliced a vulturine beak; the thing gargled and toppled. I ducked the second chain and then brought my own back so fast I nearly overbalanced. It looped around that incredibly thin and long neck, doubled on itself. I yanked and the Rapa staggered forward so that I could land a solid blow. He collapsed. I heard a shout behind me and ducked again and the chain smashed a huge chunk from the wooden side of the skiff. I sprang to face the last Rapa.

He poised, the chain circling.

His beaked face leered on me; he knew all must be over for him—and yet, could he dispose of me and row for the main canal he would be away, and with a human woman as a hostage. He had all to play for. I feinted and the chain hissed. I pulled back and he leered at me again.

"Human offal!" His gobbling croak harsh in my ears stilled the mad thumping of my heart. I sized him up. That chain could break an arm, a leg, could throttle me, long before I could reach him. I flexed my legs, braced against the bottom boards where water slopped. He had not, perhaps, the experience in boats I had. I began to rock from side to side.

His arms flew up. The chain circled crazily. The woman was clutching the transom in both hands I could not see her face for she wore a heavy veil of emerald silk. I rocked furiously. The Rapa staggered and lurched, recovered his balance, toppled the other way. The gunwales of the fragile skiff were slopping water at each roll.

With a shriek of mingled fury and despair the Rapa dropped his chain and lurched down to grab at the gunwale and with a last savage rocking motion of my leg I tipped him clean out of the boat. He flew across the water and went in face first, spread-eagled. His splash was a magnificent flower of foam. I did not laugh.

I quietened the skiff in the water and seized the oars. The Rapa drifted away. I turned to the woman.

"Well, my girl," I said harshly. "You're all right. No harm has come to you."

I did not want her to panic, lest she upset the skiff.

She regarded me through the eyeslits of her veil. She sat very still and straight. I towered above her, my naked chest heaving from the slight exertion of the fight, water and sweat riveting down my thighs where the ridged muscle shone hard, like iron.

She wore a long gown of emerald green, unrelieved by ornament. Above the green veil she wore a tricorne hat of black silk, with a curled emerald green feather. Her hands were cased in white gloves, and on three of her fingers, outside the gloves, she wore rings: one emerald, one ruby and one sapphire.

I began to pull back to the jetty.

A story to account for my broken slave chains rose into my mind.

The woman had not said anything. She sat so still, so silent, that I thought she must be in shock.

When we reached the jetty she stood up and held out a foot in its jeweled strappings. I reached out my palm and she put her foot in that brown and powerful hand and I lifted her up onto the jetty as an elevator lifts one up through the giant trunks of the plant-houses in distant Aphrasöe.

A certain concern was removed from my mind as I saw floating in the water the form of a Rapa guard with a slave chain wrapped around his neck, his great beaked face twisted sideways and loose from his trunk. He was a Deldar, a commander of ten, and he had been the sixth guard aboard our wherry.

Slowly I climbed onto the jetty

The woman was surrounded by a clamoring mob of guards and nobles in gaudy finery. Of slaves there was no sign save the blood that stained the stones beneath their feet.

"Princess!" they were calling. And: "We thought your precious light had been removed from us!" And: "Praise be to mighty Zim and to thrice-powerful Genodras that you are safe!"

She turned to face me, her head high, her gown stiff and tent-like about her, her jeweled feet invisible. She lifted a white-gloved hand and the babble fell silent

"Dray Prescot," she said, and, saying, astonished me beyond words. "You may incline to me."

I stood there in the light of the twin suns, a reddish shadow from my heels lying north-northwest and a greenish shadow lying northwest by north, give or take a point. Nowadays, of course, a ship can be steered to a degree; it is wonderful what a difference steam and diesel and nuclear power have made to navigation of the oceans— I gaped at her.

The man I remembered as Galna thrust forward. His face was at once ugly and vengeful and gloating. His all-over green leathers glistened in that Antarean sunshine.

"I shall run him through now, my Princess, as you desire."

He drew a rapier from a velvet lined sheath. I hardly

noticed the thing. I stared at the woman. Incline to her? I did not want to die. I bowed, a stiffly formal making of a leg, my right hand elegantly waving in the air before my breast and then finishing up, fingers gracefully curled; before me, my leg stuck forward, the other back, my left arm outstretched behind me, my head bowed over low— low!

If this absurd posture, so carefully taught in the scented drawing rooms of Europe, should be taken as an insult— I heard a light laugh.

"Do not kill the rast now, Galna. He will make better sport—later."

I straightened up. "I was freed from my chains by the Rapa guard so as to help better with the marble—" I began to say. Galna struck me viciously across the face with the flat of his rapier. At least, he would have done, had I not jerked my head back. Men jumped forward.

"Down, rast, when the princess addresses you."

An arm laid across my back, a foot twitched my ankles, and I was down, spine bent, rear high, nose thrust painfully into the stones of the jetty where marble dust irritated my eyes and nostrils. Four men held me.

"Incline, rast!"

Perforce, I inclined. I had learned something a slave of the Esztercari Household must know in order to stay alive.

Even then, as my nose bumped painfully in the marble dust of the jetty, I contrasted this barbarous posture with the graceful gestures of the ceremony of obi.

I knew that death was very near.

Princess Natema Cydones stirred me with her jeweled foot. Her toes were lacquered that same brilliant green.

"You may crouch, slave."

Assuming this meant exactly what it sounded like I sat up in a crouching position, like a fawning dog. No one struck me, so I guessed I had learned a little more. There had been some sharp words, and muttering, and acid commands from the group and now I heard the clink of chains. A short stout man clad in a pale gray tunic-like garment bound with emerald green borders, and with two large green key-shaped devices stitched to his breast and back, now strutted forward. Under the fuming eyes and pointed rapiers of Galna and the other nobles, this man loaded me with chains. He snapped an iron ring about my neck, an iron band about my waist, wristlets and anklets, and from loops on all of these weighty objects he strung what seemed to me more than a cable's length of harsh iron chain.

"See that he is transferred to my opal palace, Nijni," ordered the princess, casually, as though discussing the delivery of a new pair of gloves. No—as I was prodded along by the slave-master Nijni's sturm-wood wand of office, I knew I was wrong. She would give more concern, much more concern, to the choosing of a new pair of gloves.

I had escaped from one kind of slavery to that of another.

The future loomed as dark and perilous as ever. Only one ray of hope in all this I could see—my men, my loyal clansmen, my brothers in obi, had been set free from their slavery and their chains.

## Chapter Eleven

# The Princess Natema Cydones
# of the Noble House of Esztercari

How my brothers in obi would have laughed to see me now! How those fierce fanatical clansmen would have roared their mirth to see their Zorcander, their Vovedeer, dressed like a popinjay! Three days had passed since my futile attempt at escape. I knew I had been bought from the marble quarries. When the Princess Natema wanted anything men trembled for their lives until that thing was brought her. Now I strode the tiny wooden box in the attic of the opal palace I had been given as my room— strange, I had thought when a gray-clad slave girl had shown me in with a furtive, scared look—and stared at myself in contempt.

I had refused to don the garments; but Nijni, the fat, dour, ever-cham-chewing slave-master had whistled up three immense fellows—scarcely human with their bristle bullet-heads, their massively rolling shoulders, their thick dun-colored hides mantled with muscles of near-armor thickness and toughness, their short sinewy legs and slayed feet—two to hold me and the third to strike me painfully across the back and buttocks with a thin cane. This was so remarkably like the rattans carried by our warrant officers of the King's Ships on which I had served that I received three strokes before I had sense enough to cry out that I would don the garments, for, after all, what did foolish fancy dress signify in so much of squalor and misery?

The man who had struck me, and I must think of him as a man although from what pot of incestuous and savage genes he sprang I do not care to contemplate, leaned close as he went out.

"I am Gloag," he said. "Do not despair. The day will come." He spoke in, a voice throttled in his throat, a whisper from lungs and voice box used to a stentorian bellow as a normal method of conversation.

I gave no sign I had heard.

So now I looked in dissatisfaction at myself. I wore a fancy shirt of emerald and white lozenges, with scarlet embroidery. A silk pair of breeches of yellow and white, with a great embroidered cummerbund of eye-watering colors. On my head perched a great white and golden turban, ablaze with glass stones, and gay feathers, and dangling beads. I felt not only a fool, I felt a nincompoop.

If my savage brethren of the plains of Segesthes saw me now what would they not make in jest and ribald comment of their feared and respected Vovedeer?

Nijni came for me with Gloag and his men, and three lithe lissom young slave girls. The girls were clad in strings of pearls and precious little else. Gloag and his men were from Mehzta, one of the nine islands of Kregen. They wore the usual simple gray breechclout of the slave, but they each had an emerald green waistbelt, from which dangled the slim rattan cane. I went with them. In my naïveté I had no idea of where I was going, or of why I was dressed as I was, or even why I had been forced, not unpleasantly, to go through the baths of the nine. This was simply a process of proceeding from lukewarm water where the grime washed off me in sooty clouds into the liquid, through nine rooms where the water grew at each step hotter and hotter until the sweat rolled from me, and then colder and colder until I shouted and shivered and bounded as though from ice floes. I did feel invigorated, though.

Nijni paused before an ornate gold and silver door set with emeralds. From a side table he took a box and from the box a paper-wrapped bundle. Carefully he pared back the tissue. Within, virginal, white, gleaming, lay a pair of incredibly thin white silk gloves.

The slave girls with exquisite delicacy helped me don

the gloves. Nijni looked at me, chewing endlessly on his wad of cham, his head cocked on one side.

"For every rip or tear in the gloves," he said, "you will receive three strokes of the rattan. "For every soil mark, one stroke. Do not forget." Then he threw open the doors.

The room was small, sumptuous, refined past elegance, decadent. It was, I suppose, what one would expect of a princess who had been brought up from birth to have every whim instantly gratified, to have every luxury heaped on her as a right, and who had never felt the restraining touch of an older or wiser hand, or the sound common sense of a person to whom everything is not possible.

She reclined on a chaise longue beneath a golden lamp carved in the semblance of one of the graceful flightless birds of the plains of Segesthes the clansmen love to hunt and catch to give their bright feathers to the girls of the vast chunkrah herds. She wore a short gown of emerald green—that eternal hateful color—relieved by a silken vest of silver tissue. Her arms were bare, round and rosy in the light. Her ankles were neat, her calves fine, but I thought her thighs a fraction heavy, firm and round and delightful; but that infinitesimal fraction too thick for a man of my finicky tastes. Her lush yellow hair was piled atop her head and held in place by pins with emerald gems. The sweetness of her mouth shone red and warm and inviting.

Beyond her, in an alcove, I could see the lower body and feet of a gigantic man clad in mesh steel. His chest and head were hidden from view by two carved ivory swing doors. By his side, its point resting on the floor, he held a long rapier. I did not need to be told that a single command from the Princess Natema would bring him in a single bound into the room, that deadly point at my throat or buried in my heart.

"You may incline," she said.

I did so. She had not called me a rast. A rast, I knew now, was a disgusting six-legged rodent that infested dunghills. Maybe she was wrong. Maybe, apart from my four limbs and my larger size I, in this palace, was no better than a rast in his dunghill. At least, that was his nature.

"You may crouch."

I did so.

"Look at me."

I did so. In all truth, that was not a hard command to obey.

Slowly, languorously, she rose from the couch. Her white arms, rounded and rosy in the lamplight, reached up and, artfully, lasciviously, she pulled the emerald pins from her hair so that it fell in a glory around her. She moved about the room, lightly, gracefully, scarcely seeming to touch the scented rugs of far Pandahem with those pink feet with their emerald-lacquered toenails that shone so wantonly. The green gown drooped about her shoulders and I caught my breath as those two firm rounds appeared beneath the silk; lower down her arms dropped the gown, lower, sliding with a kind of breathless hiss, so that at last she stood before me clad only in the white tissue vest that ended in a scalloped edge across her thighs. Silver threads glittered through the tissue. Her form glowed within like some sacred flame within the holy precincts of a temple.

She stared down on me, insolently, taunting me, knowing full well the power and the drug of her body. Her red lips pouted at me, and the lamplight caught on them and shot a dazzling star of lust into my eyes.

"Am I not a woman, Dray Prescot?"

"Aye," I said. "You are a woman."

"Am I of all women not the most fair?"

She had not touched me—yet.

I considered.

Her face tightened on me. Her breathing came, sharper, with a gasp. She stood before me, head thrown back, hair a shining curtain about her, her whole body instinct with all the weapons of a woman.

"Dray Prescot! I said—am I of all women not the most fair?"

"You are fair," I said.

She drew in her breath. Her small white hands clenched.

She stared down on me and I became closely aware of that grim mailed swordsman half-hidden in the alcove.

Now her contempt flowed over me like sweetened honey.

"You, perhaps, know one who is fairer than I?"

I stared up at her, levelly, eye to eye. "Aye. I did, once. But she, I think, is dead."

She laughed, cruelly, mockingly, hatefully. "Of what use a dead woman to a live man, Dray Prescot! I pardon your offense—" She halted herself, and put one hand to her heart, pressing. "I pardon you," she said, again, wonderingly. Then: "Of all women living, am I not the most fair?"

I acknowledged that. I saw no reason to get myself killed for the sake of a spoiled brat's pride. My Delia, my Delia of the Blue Mountains—I thought of her then and a pang of agony touched me so that I nearly forgot where I was and groaned aloud. Could Delia be dead? Or could she have been taken by the Savanti back to Aphrasöe? There was no way I could find that out except by finding the City of the Savanti—and that seemed impossible even if I were free.

As though suddenly wearying of this petty taunting, although, heaven knew, she was prideful enough of her beauty, she flung herself wantonly on the chaise longue, her head back, her arms flung casually out, her golden hair cascading down to the rugs from far Pandahem. "Bring me wine," she said, indolently, pointing with her jeweled foot.

Obediently I arose and filled the crystal goblet with a golden, light wine I did not recognize, from the great amber flask. It did not smell particularly good to me. She did not offer me any to drink; I did not care.

"My father," she said, as though her mind had turned ninety degrees into the wind, "has a mind I should marry the Prince Pracek, of the House of Ponthieu." I did not answer. "The Houses of Esztercari and of Ponthieu are at the moment aligned and in control of the Great Assembly. I speak of these matters to you, dolt, so that you may realize I am not just a beautiful woman." Still I did not reply. She went on, dreamily: "Between us we have fifty seats. With the other Houses, both Noble and Lay, who are aligned with us, we form a powerful enough party to control all that matters. I shall be the most powerful woman in all Zenicce."

If she expected a reply she received none.

"My father," she said, sitting up and propping her rounded chin on her fist and regarding me with those luminous cornflower blue eyes. "My father, because he holds the power of the alignment, is the city's Kodifex, its emperor. You should feel extremely fortunate, Dray Prescot, to be slave in the Noble House of Esztercari."

I lowered my head.

"I think," she said, in that dreamy voice, "I will have you hung from a beam and whipped. Discipline is a good item in the agenda for you to learn."

I said: "May I speak, Princess?"

She lifted her breast in a sudden deep intake of breath. Her eyes glowed molten on me. Then: "Speak, slave!"

"I have not been a slave long. I am growing uncomfortable in this ridiculous position. If you do not allow me to stand up I shall probably fall over."

She flinched back, her brows drawing down, her lips trembling. I am not sure, even now, even after all these long years, if she truly realized she was being made fun of. Such a thing had never happened to her before—so how could she know? But she knew I had not responded as a slave should. In that disastrous moment for her she lost the semblance of a haughty princess beneath whose jeweled feet all men were a rasts. Her silver vest crinkled with the violence of her breathing. Then she snatched up her green gown and swathed it carelessly about her body and struck with her polished fingernails upon a golden gong hung on cords within arm's reach of the chaise longue.

At once Nijni and the slave girls and Gloag and his men entered.

"Take the slave back to his room."

Nijni cringed, making the half-incline.

"Is he to be punished, oh Princess?"

I waited.

"No. no—take him back. I will call for him again."

Gloag, as it seemed to me, very roughly bundled me out.

The three slave girls in their scanty strings of pearls were laughing and giggling and looking at me slyly from the corners of their slanting blue eyes. I wondered what the devil they were finding to chatter about; and then bethought me of my ludicrous clothing. I thought what Rov Kovno, or Loku, or Hap Loder, would make of them, on the backs of voves riding into the red sunset of Antares on the great plains of Segesthes.

Gloag clapped me on the back.

"At least, you still live, Dray Prescot."

We left that scented powdered corridor where Nijni removed the silken gloves from my hands. The wine had stained my right thumb. He looked up, crowing, chewing his cham-cud.

"One stroke of the rattan!" he said, annoyed it was not more. A slave girl in the drab gray breechclout of all slave menials walked around the corner before us carrying a huge earthenware jar of water. A lamp swung from golden chains beyond her head suddenly aureoled her hair and shone into my eyes. I turned my face away, glowering at Nijni.

I heard a desperate gasp. I heard the jar of water smash into a thousand pieces and the water splash and leap in that hidden corridor of a decadent palace. I looked up, moving my eyes away from the light so I could see.

Clad in the gray breechclout, her head high and face frozen, her eyes filled with tears, Delia of the Blue Mountains looked hard and long at me, Dray Prescot, clad in those foolish and betraying clothes.

Then, with a sob of anger and despair, she rushed from my sight.

## Chapter Twelve

# The Jiktar and the Hikdar

Was it truly Delia of Delphond, Delia of the Blue Mountains,?

How could it be? A slave, in the gray breechclout, was that my Delia? I was back in my little wooden room behind the ornate facade lining one of the tilting roofs of Princess Natema's opal palace. I groaned. Delia, Delia, Delia....

It must have been a girl who in that sudden lamplit illumination had reminded me of Delia. Then why had she turned from me with tear-filled eyes, why had she run from me, sobbing with anguish—or choking back her anger and scorn? In truth I did not know, so tumbled were my thoughts, just how this girl had reacted.

An over-man-size statue of a Talu, one of those mythical, as I thought, eight-armed people of the sloe-eyes and the bangles and the dances, carved all in the ivory of the mastodon trunk, had been standing on the corner beyond the lamp. It had gleamed palely ivory at me as I leaped forward. I collided with the thing and, instinctively catching it and supporting it, its eight arms a wagon wheel of wanton display about me, fingertips touching in erotic meaning, I lost sight of the girl who vanished between the mazes of colored pillars supporting the roof. A giant gong note sounded.

Nijni was puffing and chewing furiously.

"She will not escape!" he shouted, gobbling the words, beside himself. "I shall have her whipped on that fair skin—"

I took his gray tunic between my fingers, and gripped, and lifted him until the curled toes of his slippers left the carpet and he dangled in my fist. I thrust my ugly face into his.

"Rast!" I roared at him. "If you so much as have one hair of her head injured I shall break your back!"

He gobbled to speak, and could not, although his meaning was plain.

"Though you flog me a thousand and a thousand times," I snarled at him, shaking him, "I shall break your back."

I dumped him down onto the carpet where he staggered back into the arms of the slave girls who had huddled, staring at me in terror. I noticed how slowly Gloag and his men had come to the assistance of the slave-master. Now they stepped forward, whistling their rattans about their heads, and I was prepared to be taken back to my room. Here Gloag administered the single stroke I had earned by spilling wine on my silk glove. I thought his stroke oddly fierce. He whispered to me as they left.

"The time is not yet. Do not arouse their suspicions, or by Father Mehzta-Makku I'll break your back myself!"

Then he was gone.

Of course I tried to find out about the slave who had smashed and spilled the water jar; but no one would tell me anything and I fumed and fretted in that stifling room. Occasionally, wearing those infernally idiotic clothes, I would be taken out into a tree-shaded courtyard for exercise, and twice I saw the green-gowned and veiled form of a woman I surmised to be Natema watching me. No noble woman of Zenicce would venture beyond the confines of her enclave unveiled.

There were three more interviews with her, as unsatisfactory as the first, and on the last occasion she made me strip for her, a proceeding I found extraordinarily unpleasant and degrading; but necessary in light of the swordsman in the alcove and the rattans of the beings of Mehzta on guard outside the door. I gathered from the laughing comments of the pearl-strung slave girls that the princess was sizing me up and taking stock of my points as she might a zorca or a half-vove. The half-voves were the smaller and lighter and far less-fierce animals, like small voves, these people used.

Her contempt blazed on me, her scorn dripped on me, her complete disregard of me as a human being showed me how utterly she despised me. I did not care. I craved news of Delia. How Natema loved to flaunt her insolent rosy curves in my face! I sensed she was attempting to arouse me to some grand act of folly. I was not to be so lightly gulled.

Once she had Gloag and his men flog me with their rattans for no reason other, I supposed, than a girlish desire to impress me with her power. This time Gloag took it easy on me, and my skin was not broken, although it hurt damnably enough. All the time Natema stood with her lower lip caught between her teeth, her cornflower blue eyes enormous and shining, her hands clasped convulsively to her breast.

"Understand, rast, that I am your mistress, your divine lord and master! You are as nothing beneath my feet!" She stamped her jeweled foot at me, her breast heaving with the tumult of her passion. I did not smile at her, although it would have been treacherously easy a thing to do, for I thought the gesture meaningless. Nevertheless, I did say: "I trust you sleep well tonight, Princess."

She stepped forward and struck me with her dainty white hand. A blow across the face I scarcely felt, so intense were the pains from my back. I looked at her, brows lowered, chin lifted, broodingly.

"You would make an interesting slave," I said.

She whirled away, shaking with a passion that Gloag, for one, did not want to try. He and his men hustled me out and a crone with a withered face and one eye doctored my back. I'd been used to flogging as part of naval discipline and four days, with the help of ointments and rest, saw me completely recovered. Gloag had proved a friend.

"Can you use a spear?" he asked me as the crone worked on my back.

"Yes."

"Will you use one, when the time is here?"

"Yes."

He bent down to me as I lay face down on the bed of my room. His blunt, square, powerful face studied mine quizzically. Then he nodded, as though finding something that satisfied him.

"Good," he said.

The Noble House of Esztercari employed no Rapa slaves. According to the other slaves it was because the

Rapas stank in the nostrils of their mistress. This would be true. They employed no Rapa guards. There were Ochs, and the Mehztas, who were slaves but with petty powers involving the use of the rattan, and other fearsome creatures I occasionally glimpsed about the opal palace. And still I could find no word of Delia—or the girl who might be Delia of Delphond.

The palace was a warren in the manner of these immense structures built by slave-labor and accreting through the years under the varying whims of successive dynasties. I had a limited run of those corridors and halls beneath the roof; but all exits were guarded by strong detachments of Chuliks, who were born with two arms and two legs like men and who possessed faces which, apart from the three-inch long upward-reaching tusks, might have been human; but who in all else knew nothing of humanity. Their skin was a smooth oily yellow and their skulls were shaved except for a green-dyed rope of hair that fell to their waists. Their eyes were small and round and black and habitually fixed in a gaze of hypnotic rigidity. They were strong, bodies well-fleshed with fat, and they were quick. The House of Esztercari uniformed them in a dove-gray tunic with emerald green bands. Their weapons were the same as gentlemen and nobles of Zenicce—the rapier and the dagger.

The rapier is known generally as the Jiktar—commander of a thousand—and its inseparable companion the dagger as the Hikdar—commander of a hundred. Of the throwing knife men will often say, dismissingly, that it is the Deldar—the commander of ten. In this I think they make a mistake. For some strange reason the men—and the quasi-human beasts—of Segesthes are absolutely contemptuous of the shield. It is known and scorned. They seem to regard the shield as a weakling's weapon, as cowardly, sly, deceitful. Given their skill with arms, an undoubted skill as you shall hear, it is amazing to me that the manifold advantages of the aggressively-used shield are not obvious to them. Perhaps they are, and their code of honor forbids its use. Long have I argued the point, almost until my friends looked at me askance, and wondered if I were not like the shield myself, weak, cowardly, deceitful—until I have thumped them a buffet and proved them wrong in friendly combat.

By now it was clear to me what my intended role would

be as a pampered slave in the House of Esztercari. From
hints and whispers, and forthright counsels of scorn from
Gloag, I gathered that never before had the Princess
Natema been faced with a man who was not overawed
and unmanned by her beauty. She could make men crawl
on their knees to kiss her jeweled feet. She could make me
do this, too, of course, by threat of torture and flogging.
But she had always gloried in her womanly power over
men without need of other coercion.

More and more she grew tired that I would not break
to her of my own free will. I suspected if I did the mailed
swordsman would be summoned from the alcove to make
an end of me and Natema would look for her next
plaything.

No one, not even Nijni, knew how many slaves there
were in the House of Esztercari. There were books of
account, kept by slave scribes; but slaves died, were sold,
fresh slaves were bought or exchanged and the accounts
were never up-to-date. To add to the confusion, within the
Noble House itself there were many families—that of
Cydones being the Premier Family—and one might sell
a slave within the House and cross him or her off the lists;
but he was still slaving in the stables or she was fetching
water in the kitchens of one of the palaces on the Enclave
of Esztercari.

During this period the news of an encounter flew about
the slave rooms and halls. The Lay House of Parang had
been attacked across the canal separating its enclave from
that of the Noble House of Eward. Those of Eward hotly
denied their guilt, blaming others unknown. Gloag winked
at me.

That's the work of the Ponthieu, by Father Mehzta-
Makku! They hate Eward like poison, and our House
backs them."

I remembered what Natema had said of the alignment
of power.

This petty political chicanery and bravo-fighting meant
nothing to me. I hungered for Delia. And yet, I had to
face the unpalatable fact that I had no proof Delia cared
for me. How could I aspire to her, after what had happened? Had I not interfered in Aphrasöe, she might have
been cured, have been safely home with her people in far
Delphond—wherever that was. The name was known—
and I had thrilled to that information—but no slave could

tell me where it was, or if it was a continent, an island, a city.

Undoubtedly, I reasoned, Delia had every cause to hate me.

The next evening I was sent for by Natema and instead of Gloag and his Mehztas the escort consisted of yellow-skinned Chuliks, their gray tunics bright with emerald bands, and their rapiers swinging with an insolent swagger. They wore black leather boots, that clashed on the floor. A fresh consignment of Chulik mercenaries had recently arrived in Zenicce and the House of Esztercari had taken the major proportion to serve her devious ends.

The first thing I noticed as I entered that scented room with the white silk gloves upon my hands was that the steel-meshed swordsman no longer stood half-concealed in his alcove.

Steel-mesh was a rare and valuable armor in Segesthes; men habitually wore arm and leg clasps, and breasts and backs, with dwarf pauldrons, mostly of bronze; sometimes of steel. Always, the ideal of the Segesthan fighting man was attack—always, attack.

The Princess Natema looked incredibly lovely this evening as the first Kregen's seven moons floated into the paling topaz sky. Her long emerald gown was gone, and she wore a sparkling golden vestment that limned her form breathtakingly. She smiled on me and held out her arms.

"Dray Prescot!" She stamped her jeweled foot; but not in rage. A subtle transformation had turned her domineering ways aside, so that she seemed to me almost more lovely than she had been. She bade me rise from the incline—and amazingly she made me sit down at her side. She poured wine for me.

"You said I would prove an interesting slave," she whispered. Her eyes lowered. Her breast moved with the violence of her breathing. I felt most uneasy. That damned swordsman was missing, and I'd come to regard him, incredible though it may sound, as a kind of chaperon.

Our relationship, Natema's and mine, had flowered almost unnoticed by me; but clearly she believed that I was passionately drugged by her beauty and frightened only of being killed, and ready, now, to overlook that blemish in my pure regard for her. Many men had died for her, I knew. Her seduction of me progressed with a steady sure possessiveness like that of a python swallowing down its kill. I resisted, for although she was a flower of women, and immensely subtle in her dispensation of pleasure, I could think only of Delia. I do not claim any great powers of self-control; many men would regard me as a fool not to sip the honey while the blooms are open. But the more her passionate advances continued the more she, contrariwise, repelled me.

How it would have ended I do not like to think.

Strings of emeralds twined about her white throat and draggled along her naked arms as she lay on the floor at my feet, pleading unashamedly now, turning her tear-stained face up to me. Her face was flushed, hectic, passionate.

"Dray! Dray Prescot! I cannot speak your name without trembling! I want you—only you! I would be your slave girl if I could—all you want, Dray Prescot, is yours for the mere asking!"

"There is nothing between us, Natema," I said roughly.

Sink me, if I were to be killed for it I wanted nothing of this scented, evil, beautiful woman!

She ripped the golden tissue vestments from her glorious body and stretched up her arms to me, pleading, sobbing.

"Am I not beautiful, Dray Prescot? Is there a woman in all Zenicce so fair? I need you—I want you! I am a woman, you are a man—Dray Prescot!"

I backed away, and I knew then, I admit it, that I was weakening. All the passionate loveliness of her lay at my feet, all her contempt, her scorn, her taunting gone, and in their places only a beautiful distraught girl with disheveled hair and tear-streaked face begging me to love her. Oh, yes, I nearly succumbed—I was, still, at heart only a simple sailorman.

"I have watched you, Dray, many and many a time! Oh, yes! I have struggled against my desires, against my passion for you. It has torn my heart. But I cannot resist any longer." She crawled after me, begging. "Please, Dray, please!"

Could I believe her? Her words sounded like rote, like phrases learned against a need, as though she repeated them with a set purpose. And yet—naked, jewel-entwined, her rosy flesh glowing, she lay there at my feet in supplication. I did not know if this was one more damnable trick, or if she truly fancied she loved me.

She rose to her feet, her arms outstretched, her breast rising and falling with the tumult of her passion, her red lips shining, her eyes ardent with love, all her emotions rich and full and aroused—

The door smashed open and a Chulik staggered through with a thick and clumsy spear transfixing his body from which the bright blood spouted.

Natema screamed like one caught in red-hot pincers.

I leaped. I snatched up the Chulik's fallen rapier in my right hand and scooped up in the same movement his dagger in my left. I sprang before Natema and faced the broken door.

Another Chulik collapsed inward, trying to hold together the slit edges of his throat. Men and half-men boiled outside.

"Quick!" Natema grabbed my arm. Naked, she raced to the alcove where the steel-meshed warrior had once stood. A panel slid aside. We passed through and Natema gave a quick and vicious laugh of vengeful triumph at our escape—and a spear lanced through to embed itself quivering in the wood and block the closure of the secret panel.

The sound of fierce yells and the clash of steel spurred us on and we ran bounding down stone stairs in dim lamplight until we reached a landing from which many doors opened. Feet clattered down the stone stairs after us. Before one of the doors lay the body of the man in mail. He had simply been battered to death with clubs. His body was broken and pulped within the mesh. Around him lay piled bodies of slaves, both men and beast. He had died well. A door had banged as we descended and I surmised the slaves trying to pass the mailed man had heard us descending and thought we were guards come to reinforce this lone warrior. I saluted him as he deserved.

Then I bent and took off his broad leather belt with its plain steel buckle. On the belt were hung his rapier and dagger scabbards. Those two superb weapons I picked up—one from the body of an Och slave, the other from a plug-ugly with black hair all over him and a nose ten degrees to port.

"Hurry, you fool!" screamed Natema.

I ran after her, clutching my arsenal of weapons.

We passed through a door and along passageways within the palace dimly-lit with oil lamps. Shadows swung wildly about us. I heard the noise of feet ahead and halted. Natema clung to me, soft and firm and panting, her hair dangling before her face. Angrily she thrust it back. I took the opportunity to buckle the warrior's broad leather belt about my waist. The fancy clothes came in useful to wipe the blades clean; then I wadded them and tossed them aside and stood only in my breechclout.

"Nijni will not be pleased," I whispered.

"What?" She was startled.

"His white silk gloves are ruined."

"You idiot!" Her nostrils whitened. "There are killers ahead of us, and you prate of white silk gloves!"

Natema still wore emerald earrings and a single chain of gems about her neck, depending to her waist. These I took in my fingers and removed, and she stared at me with her blue eyes wide and drugged with the emotions of the moment. I threw the stones away.

"Come," I said. I looked at her. I bent, rubbed my hand in the dust of the floor and then smeared that filth all over her face and hair and body as she struggled and twisted, cursing. "Remember," I said hrashly. "You are slave."

She slew me with her eyes. Then we padded on, furtively, toward the sounds of conflict and killing, and I made very sure that the Princess Natema hung her head and dragged her heels as a docile slave should.

## Chapter Thirteen

# The fight in the passage

There were five of them in a narrow passageway that led between the slave's domestic workrooms and the noble portion of the palace on the floor immediately below that containing the princess' private boudoir. They had three slave girls for their sport and they wanted another. Natema and I had worked our way through the chaos of the palace, passing furious isolated fights, dodging aside as slaves ran and were killed by Ochs or Chuliks, and as guards ran and were slain by slaves. I had picked up a gray breechclout for Natema, and she had grimaced at the filth and bloodstains upon it; but I had spanked her where it stung and she donned the dismal garment. We insinuated ourselves through the slave-dominated areas, ever-watchful for guards; but it would have been madness to have declared Natema for who she was here; to my satisfaction, I must admit, the slaying of guards was far more in evidence than the killing of slaves and we must, perforce, wait. Although I itched to get into the fight and battle alongside my fellow slaves, I felt a curious inverted responsibility for Natema.

She could not be all evil; she might truly love me, as she said, and that at once placed a responsibility in my hands. And, even if she did not, I did not relish the thought of her radiant loveliness despoiled by the frantic army of carousing, slaying, singing slaves everywhere on the rampage.

So we worked our way through to where she promised me there would be safety, and here we were, our way barred by five Chuliks with three human girls for their sport, not joining the fighting as, being paid mercenaries, they should.

They saw Natema and laughed, their tusks gleaming, and called out.

"Let her go, slave, and you can return." And: "Give her to us and you will not be killed." And: "By Likshu the Treacherous! She is a beauty!"

I put Natema behind me. We must go ahead, to the safety of the noble apartments. The Chuliks stopped laughing. They looked puzzled. Three of them drew their rapiers and daggers.

"What, slave, would you dispute an order from your masters?"

I said softly: "You may not have this girl. She is mine."

I heard a low gasp from Natema.

The three huddled slave girls scarcely merited a glance; all my attention was on the mercenaries. Had they been Ochs the odds would have been more even. I advanced a foot and brandished the rapier and dagger as my old Spanish master had taught me so long ago.

"The French system is neat and precise," he had said. "And the Italian, also." He had taught me fine arts of fencing with the small sword, often erroneously called a rapier. With that nimble little sticker one can thrust and parry with the same blade. With the heavier, stiffer Elizabethan rapier, such a blade as I now grasped, one needed to dodge or duck a thrust, or to interpose the dagger, the rapier's lieutenant, the Hikdar to the Jiktar. Even so, I could fence well with the rapier without a main gauche. I hold no great pride in this thing; it was all of a oneness with my ability to run out along the topgallant yard in a storm, or to swim incredible distances underwater without coming to the surface for a breath. One is what one is, what is in one's nature.

Nowadays, that is in the twentieth century, foil fencing, foil-play, such as one learns at a university, is a far removed from the art of sword fighting to kill as is Earth from Kregen. *La jeu du terrain* also bears little relation to the ferocious and deadly sword combats of Kregen. Given the featherweight lightness of modern foils, the parry which avoids an electric light and bell recording a hit would be passed scarcely noticed by the rapier wielded by a duelist of Zenicce. No young cockscomb who foil-plays at a university could hope to survive on savage Kregen without a sharp and salutary alteration of his ways.

At the time of which I speak, however, most of my sword fighting had been done with cutlass aboard ship and with the broadsword or shortsword from the backs of zorca or vove. I had not fenced or used a rapier in years. All sword fighting tends from the complicated to the simple. These Chuliks because of the narrowness of the corridor, further narrowed in one place by an enormous Pandahem jar, could come at me only two at a time. Very well, then. They could die two at a time.

The blades clashed and rang between the walls. I took the first one on my dagger, twirled, twisted at the same time the second Chulik's rapier on my own, rolled my wrist, thrust, drew out the stained blade and immediately took the renewed first's attack once more on the dagger. It was all very slow. Slow, yes—but deadly.

My rapier was caught on the third opponent's blade— he stepped most gallantly over the twitching body of his companion to get at me—but before he could fairly engage I had spitted the first one through the throat, and then, springing aside, let the long lunge of the new antagonist go swishing past my side. I closed in rapidly, inside his guard, and thrust my dagger into his belly. Instantly I dragged my blades clear and sprang to meet the last two—and at the first onset my captured Chulik rapier snapped clean across with a devastating pinging.

I heard the women screaming.

Blood made the floor slippery. I hurled the broken hilt at a Chulik, who dodged nimbly. His yellow face slicked under the lamplight. The fray was close and deadly for a moment as my dagger held them at bay, and then I had drawn the rapier I had taken from the mailed warrior—he who had fought so nobly and died so well.

Indeed, and his blade was a marvel! The balance, the deftness of it, the suppleness as the gleaming steel whickered between the ribs of the penultimate antagonist!

The last one stared in appalled horror on the four dead bodies of his carousing-companions. He tried to escape. I would have let him go. I stepped aside for him in the corridor and raised my blood-stained blade in ironic salute. My eye caught a movement to the side and I glanced quickly to see the three slave girls rising. Two were still partly draped in strings of pearls. Trust these mercenary ruffians to select the prettiest and most pleasure-skilled of slave girls. Then I saw the third—naked, trembling, but with eyes filled with a fire I knew and remembered and loved—Delia, my Delia. . . .

Natema shouted, shrilly, her voice filled with terror.

I flicked my glance back. The Chulik whom I had been about to let go, with the honors of battle, had seen my involuntary look toward the girls, and he had stepped in and was in the act of thrusting his rapier between my ribs. My opinion of him as a fighting man went down. He should, in those close quarters, have used his dagger. Had he done so I would not now be telling you this. I flicked the long blade away with my own dagger and sank my rapier into his belly. He writhed for a moment on the brand; then I withdrew it and he slumped, vomiting, to the floor.

Natema rushed to me and clasped me, shaking and sobbing.

"Oh, Dray! Dray! A true fighting man of Zenicce, worthy of the Noble House of Esztercari!"

I tried to shake her off.

I stared at Delia of the Blue Mountains, who drew herself up, naked and grimed, her hair dusty and bedraggled, her body taut and firm in the lamplight. She looked at me with those limpid brown eyes and—was it anguish, I saw? Or was it contempt, and anger, and a sudden cold indifference?

I was standing by that great jar of Pandahem porcelain.

We were abruptly surrounded by green clad nobles who surged into the corridor, chief among them Galna, whose hard white face ridged and planed as he saw Natema. He cried out in horror and whisked a fellow-noble's gaudy cape about her glowing nakedness. The slave girls were hustled back with the rest of us as the princess was placed within a solid palisade of noble living flesh. There was some confusion.

Galna saw me.

His eyes were always mean; but now they narrowed and the hardness and meanness drilled me. He lifted his rapier.

"Galna! Dray Prescot is—" Natema stopped. Her voice lifted again, once more arrogant, once more assured, the mistress of the utmost marvels of Kregen. "He is to be treated well, Galna. See to it."

"Yes, my Princess." Galna swung back to me. "Give me your sword."

Obediently I handed across the nearest Chulik sword I had already picked up against this moment. I also handed across the Chulik dagger that had not, like its Jiktar, failed me. Now my breechclout concealed the broad belt, and the scabbard flapped against my legs, empty. Galna let me keep those, as he supposed, tawdry souvenirs of my struggle.

I tried to hurry after Delia; but there was much coming and going in the barricaded nobles' quarters as arrogant young men, gentlemen, officers, bravos, from Esztercari and from Ponthieu and many of the Houses who were aligned with those two Houses' axis, congregated for the great hunt and slaying of slaves that was to ensue. I lost Delia. I was ordered by Natèma to take the baths of nine and then to go to my room. As though I were some infant midshipman caught in a childish prank, banished to the masthead!

"I will send for you, slave," were her farewell words to me. I didn't give a tinker's cuss for her. Delia ... Delia!

Natema for the sake of her dignity and position must display her pride and arrogance before all men. She could not own to anyone the love for a slave she had only recently been so ardently displaying to me, naked and begging on her knees. But when she would send for me—what could I do, say?

A knock sounded on my door, rather, a furtive scratching that lacked the courage to knock loudly. When I opened it Gloag stumbled in, his body blood-stained, his face ghastly, his fist still gripping the stump of a spear. He looked at me.

"Was this the day, Gloag?"

. He shook his head. "They brought their airboats, flying to the roof, they brought men onto our rear, men and beasts and mercenaries—swords and spears and bows—we did not have a chance." He sagged, exhausted.

"Let me bathe your wounds."

He wrenched his lips back. "This is mostly accursed guards' blood."

"I am pleased to hear it."

He did not say what had brought him here. He did not need to. This man had struck me with the rattan. I fetched water in a bowl, and salves left by the old crone

for his wounds and bruises, and fresh towels, and I
cleaned him up. Then I pulled my trundle bed away from
the wall and pointed to the space beneath it, between wall
and floor.

He grasped my hand. His great booming voice husked.

"Mehzta-Makku, Father of all, shine down in mercy
upon you!"

I said nothing but pushed the bed back, concealing him.

The killing of slaves went on for three days in the opal
palace of the Princess Natema Cydones of the Noble
House of Esztercari. Many were the brilliantly-colored
liveries of the different Houses in alignment with Esztercari as they came hurrying to suppress this slave revolt.
The city wardens in their crimson and emerald also acted
with vigor; for this was a matter that touched the security
of the whole city of Zenicce.

During this period I brought food and wine for Gloag,
hidden beneath my bed, and saw to his toilet needs, and
talked to him, so that we came to understand each other
better.

"I hear you are a great swordsman with rapier and
dagger," he said, licking his bowl with a crust.

"I could show you a style of fence with a smaller sword
than a rapier, without a dagger, that would astonish these
rufflers."

"You would teach me swordplay?"

"Do you know the layout of the palace?"

Gloag did; he might know little of the city, but he could
find his way about the opal palace readily enough by its
secret warrens and runnels. He had not escaped before
because his duty lay with the slaves; now he was trapped
in my room. I promised him.

I believe that only Delia and the two slave girls in their
strings of pearls, Gloag and myself, and one other, escaped the dreadful retribution wrought upon the slaves.
When all had been killed the Noble House spent of their
fortune to buy more slaves. That hurt them—the sheer
financial loss on the slave revolt.

Natema sent for me and, once more dressed in my
offensive clothes, a new set even more luxurious than the
last with a great deal of brilliant scarlet, I went with
guards and Nijni—who as slave-master held a post of
some authority and had hidden during the revolt—up to a
high roof overlooking the broad arm of the delta on its

seaward side. Wide-winged gulls circled overhead. The suns sparkled off the water, and the air smelled fresh and sharp with sea-tang after the close sickly confinement of the palace. I opened my lungs and drew in that old familiar odor.

Landward of us lay the city, a blaze of color and light, with tall spires, domes, towers, battlements, creating a haphazard jumble of perspectives. Across the canal the purple and ocher trappings of the House of Ponthieu flamed from a hundred flagstaffs. Beyond their walls there were other enclaves built upon the islands of the delta. Seaward I could see—and how my heart leaped—the masts of ships moored to jetties hidden by the walls and the intervening roofs.

This hidden roof garden rioted in a thousand perfumed blooms, shady trees bowed in the breeze, marble statuary stood in niches of the walls where vines looped, water fountains tinkled. Natema waited for me reclining in a swinging hammock-type seat facing a rail overlooking a sheer drop of a thousand feet. Gulls whirled there, shrieking.

Delia of Delphond, clad in pearls and feathers, crouched by her jeweled feet.

I kept my face expressionless. I had sized up the situation instantly, and the danger made me tremble for Delia.

For Delia had uttered a low gasp at sight of me, and Natema's proud patrician face had turned to her, a tiny frown indenting her forehead above her haughty nose.

The interview wended its way as I had expected. My refusal astonished Natema. She bade her slaves retire out of earshot. She regarded me tempestuously, her hair ruffling in the breeze, her cornflower blue eyes hot and languorous, together, so that she seemed very lovely and desirable.

"Why do you refuse, Dray Prescot? Have I not offered you everything?"

"I think," I said carefully, "you would have me killed."

"No!" She clasped her hands together. "Why, Dray Prescot, why? You fought for me! You were my champion!"

"You are too beautiful to die in that way, Princess."

"Oh!"

"Would you offer me all this if I were not your slave?"

"You are my slave, to do with as I will!"

I did not answer. She looked back to where Delia sat, idly sewing a silken bit of tapestry, and pretending not to look at us. Her cheeks were flushed. Natema's ripe red mouth drew down. "I know!" she said, and her voice hissed between her white teeth. "I know! That slave wench— Here! Guards—bring me that wench!"

When the Chuliks stood grasping Delia before us, she lifted her little chin and regarded Natema with a look so proud and disdainful all my blood coursed and sang through my body. Delia did not look at me.

"This is the reason, Dray Prescot! I saw, in the corridor where you slew the five treacherous guards! I saw."

She gave an order that froze me where I stood. A Chulik drew his dagger and placed it to Delia's breast, over her heart. He looked with his oily yellow face to Natema, stolidly awaiting the next order.

"Does this girl mean anything to you, Dray Prescot?"

I stared at Delia, whose eyes now remained firmly fixed on me, her head lifted, her whole beautiful body taut and desirable and infinitely lovely. Queen among women is Delia of the Blue Mountains! Immeasurably the most beautiful woman in all Kregen and all Earth, incomparable, radiant, near-divine. I shook my head. I spoke roughly, contemptuously.

"A slave girl? No—she means nothing to me."

I saw Delia swallow and her eyelids blinked, once.

Natema smiled, like one of those she-leem of the plains, furred, feline, vicious, against which the clansmen wage continual war in protection of the chunkrah herds. She gestured and Delia returned once more to her tapestry. I noticed her fingers were not quite steady as she guided the needle; but her back was erect, her body taut, the pearls taking all their luster from the glowing glory of her skin.

"For the last time, Dray Prescot—will you?"

I shook my head, thankful that, at least for the time, Delia had been spared from immediate danger. What happened next was quick, brutal and, given the circumstances, expected.

The Chuliks at Natema's fierce, broken-voice command, seized me, ran me to the rail, thrust me half-over where I hung suspended over that gulf. Below me the water curled away from the long sandspit tailing at the end of the island. The air smelled very sweet and fresh, tanged with salt.

"Now, Dray Prescot! One word! One word is all I ask!"

I was not such a fool as to imagine I might easily survive such a dive; it would be a gamble with the odds heavily against me. I could easily throw these Chuliks off, snatch a rapier, fight my way through them and hope to escape into the warrens of the palace. But I did not think Natema would have me tossed into eternity. And, thinking that, I realized I was a fool, that she had been accustomed to doing anything at all and having anything she wanted from birth. But, if she did fancy she loved me, would she destroy me?

I braced myself, ready to twist like a zorca and fling these two yellow-bellies into space.

"One word, Natema, one word I spare you! *No!*"

I heard Delia screaming, and the scuffling sounds of a struggle. I dragged up one arm and the Chulik gasped and tried to hold me down. I was ready to turn and rend them. . . .

"What is going on here?"

The voice was harsh, strong with the tone of habitual absolute authority. The Chuliks hauled me back inboard. A tableau was frozen on that scented roof garden.

All the slaves were at the incline. Delia was held down by two Chuliks. Natema was gracefully inclining her head in a semblance of a curtsey. The man to whom these obvious and immediate marks of servile respect were addressed must be Natema's father, the Head of the House, the Cydones Esztercari, the Kodifex of the city himself.

He was tall, gaunt, with a grim pucker in the lines around his mouth, an arrogant black light in his eyes. His hair and beard were iron-gray. He stood tall, clad all in the Esztercari emerald, a jeweled rapier and dagger at his side, and I wondered how many slaves he had had killed, how many men he had spitted in duel and bravo-fight. In his face showed clearly the fanatical obsession of power, the greed to possess power and to exercise it ruthlessly.

"It is nothing, Father."

"Nothing! Do not seek to fob me off, daughter. Has the slave interfered with your girl? Tell me, Natema, by the blood of your mother."

"No, Father." Natema resumed her natural arrogant stance. "The girl means nothing to him. He has said so."

The hooded black eyes pierced into me, into Delia, into

his daughter. His hands, gloved, gripped the weapon hilts.

"You are pledged to the Prince Pracek of Ponthieu. He is here to speak to you of the wedding arrangements. I have, as is proper, attended to the financial bokkertu."

A man stepped forward from the mass of emerald green clothing in the rear of the Kodifex. I saw Galna there, his face as white and mean as ever. This young man wore the purple and ocher of Ponthieu. His rapier was over-ornate. He took Natema's hand and raised it to his forehead. He had a sharp-featured face, with that kind of lopsidedness to it that offends some people; but he was most polite.

"Princess Natema, star of heaven, beloved of Zim and Genodras, the crimson and emerald wonders of the sky—I am as dust beneath your feet."

She made some formal icy reply. She was looking at me. The Kodifex saw that look. He gestured and men—human men—seized me and Delia. They hustled us to stand before the Kodifex. Natema cried out. He silenced her.

"Do not think I am not aware of what the frippery this slave wears means, daughter! By your mother's blood, do you think I am a fool! You will obey! All else is nothing!" He gestured, a familiar, habitual movement. "Kill the man, and the girl, kill both the slaves. *Now!*"

## Chapter Fourteen

# Delia, Gloag and I
# eat palines together

"Kill both the slaves. *Now!*"

I kicked the noble Kodifex in the place where it would do him the least good, dragged the two guards around before me and hurled them staggering into the emerald green knot of nobles, snatched the Kodifex's rapier from its scabbard, slew the two guards holding Delia with two quick and savage thrusts, and seized her hand in my free left hand and dragged her running toward the stairs at the end of the roof garden.

"Dray!" she said, sobbing. "*Dray!*"

"Run, Delia of the Blue Mountains," I said. "*Run!*"

At the foot of the stairs where the doorway, ornate this side, plain the other, separated the noble area from the slave quarters beneath the roof, two Ochs tried to stop me and died for their pains. I slammed the door shut after us. We ran.

Slaves moving about their business stared at us with lackluster eyes. The buyers of the new slaves and the slave-masters like Nijni had beaten many backs right from the start so as to instill from the outset that fear and despair that is the necessary condition of the slave. We were not molested, scarcely remarked. I hoped that in a month or so the slaves would have found some semblance of the usual slavish chatter and hubbub and quick interest.

"Where are we going, Dray? What are we to do?"

I wanted to fall on my knees before this radiant girl and beg her forgiveness. But for me she would be home in Delphond, happy in the bosom of her family. How she must regard me with contempt and loathing! And, even worse, because I had been suspected of loving her she would have been killed! How often can that be said of a man's unwanted attentions to a girl on Earth?

"Hurry," I said, not trusting myself to say more.

In my room I rolled the trundle bed away. Gloag stared up. He saw Delia. His eyes went big. He saw the rapier. He whistled.

"Come, Gloag, my friend," I said, speaking with a harsh ruthlessness that made him jump up and Delia flinch.

Out we sped into the warren of passageways and halls. In an alcove far from my room I ripped off the stupid finery and between us with the rapier we cut it up and fashioned breechclouts for Gloag and myself and a tunic shift for Delia. I felt a warm admiration for the way in which she had completely accepted her nakedness in our presence. On matters as desperate as those on which we were engaged the sight of a few inches of pink skin mattered little.

We stood ready to venture forth. Delia went to hurl the strings of pearls away in disgust; but I restrained her. I put them to my teeth.

"They're real. They will serve a purpose."

Then a thought of shocking impropriety hit me. Natema as a proud princess would not clothe her slave girls in imitation pearls, it would be tasteless and loutish behavior. Would, then, she likewise clothe the man she hoped to make her paramour in imitation gems? I fancy my fingers shook a trifle as I rummaged through the pile of discarded clothing, the immense turban, the jeweled sash and slippers.

The gems were real.

I knew. I had not boarded prizes among the battlesmoke for the glory of it. I had been to a London jeweler and had handled the gems, precisely against that need.

I held a fortune in my hands.

"Hurry," I said, and thrust the gems in a fold of cloth within my breechclout. Around my waist was buckled the broad leather belt of the steel-meshed warrior. We padded down corridors known to Gloag. He carried a billet of wood. I would not much like to stop that with my cranium.

On Gloag's tough dun-colored hide, over his left shoulder blade, I had noticed a brand-mark, the solid block-lettered outlines of the Kregish letters for "C.E." Natema would not disfigure the slave maidens who attended her and whom she would see every day, and to my infinite relief Delia, having been in the kitchens only for a day, she told me, had not been branded. As the princess' potential lover and then a corpse, I, too, had not been branded.

We made sure that not a scrap of emerald green cloth remained of the fancy clothes in the material we chose for our new clothing. I slung a short scarlet square from my shoulders as a cape, and I forced Gloag to do likewise.

He knew his way with unerring accuracy, and I had navigated my way from the roof garden to my room, and so now I navigated my way alongside Gloag until we reached a narrow, dusty, cobwebby, fiang-infested corridor low in the palace where water seeped oozing through the cracks between the massive basalt blocks of the walls on one hand. We would have a better chance at night, when the twin suns have set in their riot of topaz and ruby and, if we were lucky, with a little cloud to drift between the first of the seven moons. Like any sailor, once I knew the state of tide or moon I kept that information continually turning in my head, ready at any moment to bring forth the exact state of either. On Kregen, there were seven moons with their phases to consider; but I was automatically sure that I could tell when the darkest period of the night would occur.

Accustomed to long periods on duty without food, I was concerned over Delia; but then Gloag astonished us all by producing a length of loaf, somewhat limp and bent, and a handful of palines he had kept over from the previous meal I had smuggled to him. We ate with a gusty hunger, not leaving a crumb.

Given the circumstances the rest of our escape was not overly difficult. We crawled through a stinking conduit and postern. Gloag was a superb scout. We swam the canal, stole a skiff, rowed in the dim light of three of the smaller moons passing low overhead. The nearer moons of Kregen have an appreciable motion. To escape from the city would be out of the question without an airboat, and even then the city wardens would patrol the air lanes. I asked directions, discreetly, of slaves, and Gloag it was who discovered the exact whereabouts among the islands of the enclave of Eward. I was taking a desperate gamble; but I had a card to play.

The city would be up over the escape of slaves, particularly from the ruling House, and we might simply be handed straight back. But I did not think so. Eward and Esztercari were at daggers drawn. We rowed quietly up to the stone jetty where men in the powder blue livery of Eward escorted us to an interview with the Head of their House. I had acted with arrogant authority, letting the guards see the tangible reality of my presence. A Vovedeer can be as autocratic and dictatorial as any other man who commands men, when the need arises.

Our interview was informal and pleasant. Wanek of the family of Wanek of the Noble House of Eward reminded me of no one more vividly than Cydones of Esztercari. Both men contained that gaunt obsessive drive for power. He sat in his powder blue robes, hand on fist, listening. When I had finished he called for wine, and slave girls to care for Delia.

"I welcome you to Eward, Dray Prescot," Wanek said, as we sat down to the wine and a meal. The suns were breaking in golden and crimson glory patinaed with a paler green fire in the dawn above the rooftops. "My son, the Prince Varden, is away at this time. But I shall be honored to help you. We are not as the rasts of Esztercari." His fingers gripped his chin, whitening about the knuckles. "This union between their princess and the puppy Pracek you speak of is serious." And then he began a long discourse on the tangled power politics of the city.

The General Assembly sat continuously. Never was there a break in their deliberations and debates and legislation. There were four hundred and eighty seats in the Assembly. In the city there were twenty-four Houses, both Noble and Lay, so that the average number of seats per House was twenty. Some, like Esztercari, boasted more, twenty-five, the same number as Eward. But the pressures came from alignments of power, alliances and pacts between House and House so that a party might always have the majority vote. When I marveled at the stamina of the Assemblymen Wanek laughed, and explained that only the seats counted. Anyone from a House could sit in the seats reserved to his House in the Assembly. Only the number of seats conferred the power; the men who sat in them came and went, continuously, often on a rota basis, like our system of watches at sea.

"And the Esztercari carry the weight, the alignments, and Cydones Esztercari is Kodifex of all Zenicce!"

Clearly, this was the source of the rancor in Wanek of Eward. Clearly, in his eyes, he should be Kodifex, the acknowledged leader of the most powerful coalition.

Then I saw another of the interesting facts of life in Zenicce. A bent, wizened, bearded fellow in the gray breechclout of the slave was summoned and he, with a delicacy marvelous to see, removed the brand-mark from Gloag's shoulder. He would have heated his irons and branded Gloag afresh, with the entwined "W.E." but I prevented him.

"Gloag is free," I said.

Wanek nodded. "Evidently, you and Delia of the Blue Mountains are free, Dray Prescot, for you are not branded. And so therefore must be your friend, Gloag." He motioned the brand-remover away. "I will have his skin doctored. The scar will not show." He chuckled, an unlikely sound, and yet fitting in context. "We are old hands at removing brands and substituting our own, in Zenicce."

His wife, upright, stern, yet still bearing an unmistakable aura of vanished beauty shining about her motherly virtue, said gently: "There are about three hundred thousand free people in Zenicce, compared with seven hundred thousand in the great Houses. Of course"—she gestured with one ivory-white hand—"they have no seats in the Assembly."

"They live on islands and enclaves split by avenues," said Wanek. "They ape our ways. But they are merchants and tradesmen, like ourselves, and sometimes they are useful."

I had the sense not to remark that from his words one might assume those in the Houses might not be free. Within the Houses all those not slaves were free with a freedom denied to those independent free outside.

Toward the center of the city the river Nicce divided once more in its serpentine windings to the sea and left a larger island than any other in the complex of land and water. On this island was situated the heart of the city—

the buildings of the General Assembly, the city wardens' quarters, administrative buildings, and a mind-confusing maze of small alleyways and canals off which opened the souks where anything might be bought or sold. The noise was deafening, the colors superb, the sights astounding and the smells prodigious.

After a time when it seemed that Wanek and his wife had nothing better to do than talk to me, Wanek asked, most politely, if he might inspect my rapier. I did not tell him I had taken it from Cydones Esztercari. He took it with a reverence strange to me—he could have bought and discarded a thousand like it—and then his mouth drooped.

"Inferior work," he said, looking across at his wife with a small smile. She tut-tutted, interested in her husband's occupation.

"Krasny work. But the hilt is fashionable although too cluttered with gems for a fighting man." He shot a look at me as he spoke. I rubbed my fingers.

"I had noticed," I said.

"We Ewards are the best and most renowned sword-smiths in all the world," he said, matter-of-factly.

I nodded.

"My clansmen obtain their weapons from the city, as needs they must; we do not care who fashions them provided they are the best we can buy—or take."

He rubbed his chin and handed the rapier back. "The weapons we make for sale to the butchers and tanners, who sell them to you for meat and hides, are never rapiers. Shortswords, broadswords, axes—rapiers, no."

"The man who owned this is not dead," I said. "But he is probably still doubled-up and vomiting."

"Ah," said Wanek of Eward, wisely, and asked no more.

The talk drifted. I suppose they, like a number of persons in authority, did not realize that other people were tired when they were not. The hated name of Esztercari cropped up again, and I learned they were the leading shipowners of the city. That figured. Then Wanek's wife said something almost below her breath, about the damned butchers stealing what was not theirs, and murder, and then I heard a name spring out, hard and strong and resounding.

Strombor, was the name.

I believe, now, that then, when I first heard that name

it rang and thundered in my ears with a clarion call—or do I deceive myself and am I influenced by all the intervening years? I do not know; but the name seemed to soar and echo and resound in my skull.

At last I managed to make my leave—the question of payment for their hospitality had delicately been raised and as delicately dropped—and I was conducted to a chamber where Gloag snored away in the corner. I dropped on the bed and sank into sleep and my last thought was, inevitably, of Delia of the Blue Mountains. As it was on every night of my life.

We roused in the late afternoon and satisfied our hunger with the fresh light crispy bread of Kregen, loaves as long as rapiers, and thin rashers of vosk-back, and palines, with the Kregen tea—full-bodied, aromatic, pungent—to finish. When we saw Wanek again he greeted us kindly. I asked for Delia.

"I will ask her to join us," said Wanek, and a slave departed—only to come back with the word that Delia was not in her room and the slave who had with such kind care and attention insisted on attending to her was also missing. I sat up. My hand fell to the hilt of the rapier.

"Please!" Wanek looked upset. A search was instituted; but Delia was not to be found. I raged. Wanek was beside himself at the insult he was thus forced to endure—the insult to him in that he insulted an honored guest.

Delia of the Blue Mountains and I had exchanged only a few words during our escape, for Gloag was near and, at least on my part, I felt a constraint, sure that she hated and detested me for what I had done to her. She had said something that puzzled me mightily. When we had both vanished from the pool of baptism in far Aphrasöe she had opened her eyes to find herself on the beach with the Fristles bearing down upon her, so that she had not been surprised to see me. When I had, in the moment of victory, been tumbled from the zorca, she had been taken to the city and straight to the House of Esztercari. Because of their shipping interests the Esztercari did a thriving business in slaves, and they could also command those caught in other ways. Then Delia had shaken me. For, she said, *the very next day,* she had seen me in that corridor, dressed in those accursed clothes, and had spilled and broken the water jar.

She also told me that one each of those occasions when

she had been captured or enslaved she had seen a white dove flying high, with a great scarlet and golden raptor far above.

A messenger was announced. A bluff, moustached bulky man looking oddly out-of-place in the powder·blue of the Ewards stalked in, his rapier clamped to his side, his face alive with wrath and baffled fury. He was, I understood, the House Champion, a position occupied in Esztercari by Galna of the white face and mean eyes.

"Well, Encar?"

"A message, my leader, from—from the Esztercari. A slave whom we trusted—how they mock us for that!—has abducted the Lady Delia of the Blue Mountains—"

I leaped to my feet, my blade half out of its scabbard, my hands trembling, and I know my face, ugly as it is, must have seemed diabolical to those around me.

It was true. The slave wench with her blandishments had arranged it all. She was a spy for Natema. She had got a message out, it seemed clear, and men had been waiting in that damned emerald livery at a tiny postern. There they had snatched my Delia, thrown a hood over her head, carried her swiftly aboard a gondola and poled away to the enclave of Esztercari. It was all true, heart-breakingly true.

But there was more.

"Unless the man called Dray Prescot freely surrenders himself to the Kodifex," Encar went on, his bluff honest face reflecting the distaste he felt at his words, "the Lady Delia of the Blue Mountains will meet a fate such as is meted out to recalcitrant slaves, to slaves who escape—" He faltered and looked at me.

"Go on."

"She will be stripped and turned loose into the Rapa court."

I heard gasps. I did not know—but I could guess.

"Dray Prescot—what can you do?" asked Gloag. He had risen to stand by me, splayfooted, incredibly tough, intelligent, a friend despite his dun bristly hide.

As I may have indicated, I do not laugh easily. I threw back my head, I, Dray Prescot, and laughed, there in the Great Hall of the House of Esztercari.

"I will go," I said. "I will go. And if a hair of her head is injured I will raze their House to the ground and slay them all, every last one."

## Chapter Fifteen

# In the leem pit

Gloag wanted to fight for me.

"No," I said.

"Give me a spear," he growled in that rumbling voice. "It is my business."

"Your business is my business. At least, a spear."

"You will be killed."

"I know the warrens. Without me, you will be killed."

"I know," I said.

"Then we will both be killed. Give me a spear."

I turned to Wanek, leader of the Noble House of Eward.

"Give my friend a spear."

"Now may the light of Father Mehzta-Makku shine on us both."

From Wanek I obtained a high-quality rapier and dagger, and in return told him who had been the last owner of the rapier I bore.

His delight at holding the trophy wrested from his hated enemy was keen.

"You said the hilt has value," I said. "And, here, will you keep these gems in trust for me?" I handed over the cloth-enfolded gems. Gloag insisted his share, also, should be handed over, and then I knew he meant business, for with that wealth he could have set himself up in a small way in business in the free section of the city and lived out his life in prosperity and respect.

When I told Wanek what further I requested of him he slapped his thigh in merriment, and called Encar to ready a skiff in which would go one of his men disguised to look as much like me as possible. We then went up to the roof and not without a tremor I lay down on an airboat. This was the first time I had been in one; the first time I had ever flown. Such a thing was a marvel to me. It was petal-shaped, with a transparent windshield in front, and straps to retain one in place and pelts and silks to cover the rider. Gloag and I strapped down. The driver—the word pilot was unknown to me then—except in the connotation of a ship's pilot—sent the little craft leaping into the air into the floods of sunset light from the crimson sun. The green sun would soon follow. In the course of time, after the suns' eclipse, the green sun would precede the red in order of rising and setting. The Kregan calendar is based on the suns' mutual rotations to a great extent. I braced myself as we skimmed through that ruddy falling light.

I had planned to descend on the roof garden before the skiff bearing the pseudo-me reached the Esztercari landing stage. We slanted down and, thankfully, I saw the garden empty beneath us. Gloag and I leaped off and the airboat withdrew to a discreet distance. We raced for that stairway and so into the slave quarters. Wearing the slave breechclout of grimy gray we would still attract attention by reason of our weapons, so I had elected to retain my scarlet breechclout and scarlet cape, and Gloag had done likewise. Often I have been able to pass in disguise suddenly devised where, say, a man with red or green hair would find it impossible to go, although in the House of Esztercari green dyed hair, where it was not shaved off, was common.

We found a slave girl who under the threat of Gloag's spear was only too anxious to tell us that the prisoner, whom she remembered well, was shut in the cage above the leem pit. I shuddered. Bad enough it had been to plunge once again into that towering pile of the opal palace; but far worse was it to know that we must venture down itno the depths, below the water level, where the leems slunk, furry and feline and vicious, around the damp walls of their pit. Many human bones moldered there. The leem is eight-legged, sinuous like a ferret or a weasel, but the leopard-size, with wedge-shaped head and fangs that can strike through oak. We killed them without compunction on the great plains as they sought to raid the chunkrah herds, going for preference for the young; for a grown chunkrah will impale them on his horns and hurl them a hundred yards, spitting and mewling through the air.

I have seen a blow from a leem paw with claws extended rip a warrior's head from his body and squash it like a rotten pumpkin.

Yet the leems would be far more preferable a fate for my Delia of the Blue Mountains than to be tossed nude into the Rapa court.

Our only chance was the speed and audacity of our venture.

I hoped that Cydones Esztercari and his evil daughter, the Princess Natema, would be awaiting with Galna at the landing stage the arrival of the skiff that would surely be reported to them. Yet—was Natema evil? If she truly loved me, and given the circumstances of her birth and upbringing so unfortunate as to character, would she not have acted exactly as she had done? A woman scorned is not a person to turn one's back upon, especially when she wields a dagger or can hurl a terchick.

We circled warily around the high ledge above the leem pit. The walls exuded moisture cloudy with nitrates. The place stank of leem, that close, furry, throat-clogging stench that is so noticeable in confined spaces and that is dispersed on the plains by the wind, to be scented by the savage chunkrah and warn them it is time to tail-lock, and with infants in the center, to face horn outward.

A large fully-grown leem can pull down a zorca.

A vove and two leems present so fightful a picture of mutual destruction in combat that its hideousness is best left to the imagination. I have witnessed it, and testify that truth. A vove will win, for a vove is a terrible machine of destruction; but he will need careful nursing for days thereafter, if the leems fought well.

These were the creatures who circled the walls of the pit beneath us. In the center, hanging suspended, was the cage in which Delia slumped, her wrists bound. Lines led to the cage through blocks by which means it could be pulled in and out. When Delia saw us she cried out, and the leems below hissed and spat and leaped in graceful vicious arcs up the walls of the pit.

There were six cords and I laid my hands on the one I could see would haul in the cage.

Gloag laid his spear across my arms.

"No," he said. I looked at him. "My Lady!" he called to Delia. "You must stand up and lock your arms in the bars of the cage. Hold on tightly—for your life!"

I hesitated no longer. "Do as Gloag says!"

Stumbling, her hair falling across her face, Delia stood and wedged her bound arms between two bars, hung onto a crossbar. "I am ready, Gloag," she said. Her voice did not falter.

I hauled in.

The instant the line tautened the bottom of the cage parted along the center and flapped down in two halves. Had Delia been meekly standing there she would have been pitched out like coal from a dumper, to plummet down to the fangs and claws of the leems.

I hauled her in and caught her in my arms and lowered her to the ledge. She still wore the scarlet breechclout. She trembled, suddenly, uncontrollably, and I lifted her up and a single slice of the rapier freed her from her bonds. Then we were hurrying and slipping and sliding around the ledge and out of that infernal pit.

Lamplight streaked across the sweat slicked on Delia's smooth long back and cupped in the hollows at the base of her spine. We reached the roof and the green sun had sunk; now the largest moon of Kregen, the maiden with the many smiles, sailed above us drenching the garden in a cool pink haze. The airboat driver was on the alert and came slanting in. Another airboat was approaching; the two were on converging courses. The night breeze rustled the blooms which had closed their petals at sunset and were now opening their larger outer rim of petals to the moonlight, and there were footsteps on the stairs, and voices, and harsh torchlight and the flicker of swords and daggers.

Our airboat touched. The second dropped beside it and Chuliks bounded out, their gray and emerald a weird sheen under the light. Men boiled out onto the roof behind us.

I pushed Delia toward the airboat and Gloag with his spear low made a dead run for the Chuliks.

Men behind, Chuliks before; we were outnumbered and trapped; but we would fight.

I slew three with quick simple passes, backing toward the airboats. Chuliks were attempting to get at Gloag, who passed his spear, and lunged and returned, with a wild exultant precision; but he was bringing their life's blood out to stain the flowers a more sinister color. I caught Delia around the waist with my left arm, the dagger dabbling her breast with blood.

"Up into the airboat, Gloag!" I yelled. "Hold them off from there with that damn long implement of yours!"

With a shout he leaped. The driver was now in action, his sword a glitter of fire beneath the moon. We were being pressed. Chuliks slid before me, and I battled on. Delia squirmed against my arm.

"Let me go, you great ninny!"

I released her and she scooped a dropped dagger, plunged it into the heart of a Chulik who would have taken that opportunity to do the same to me, and sprang for the Chulik airboat. The next Chulik was dispatched by me with a single thrust. I jumped for the airboat, bundling in alongside Delia, turning like a leem to slice my blade down on an upturned face, beating down his rapier guard and biting deep into his skull. An arrow caromed from the windshield. I yelled, deep and fierce, and Gloag's driver sent his craft swinging upward. The driver of the Chulik airboat, a soft-looking young man in Esztercari green, stared at my blade, gulped, and passed his hands over his controls. We began to rise. Pink moonlight fell about us. The breeze caught at my scarlet cape.

A hand grasped the gunwhale of the craft, tipping it. A Chulik rose into view, his dagger between his teeth, his rapier leaping for Delia. I brought my blade down overhand onto his head, splitting it, and he shrieked once; his hand flung up and the dagger spun away, and he fell back and wrenched the rapier, wedged in the bones of his skull, from my hand.

A long soft groan like a small explosion sounded from the airboat and whirled and all the world jumped into my throat. Delia . . . ?

An arrow had struck the driver, passing through him, and a shower more, passing where my head had been, tinkled and feathered into his controls. The airboat leaped wildly.

It rose like a cork, swinging, the wind catching it and driving it under the moonlight.

Faintly, far below, I could hear shouts.

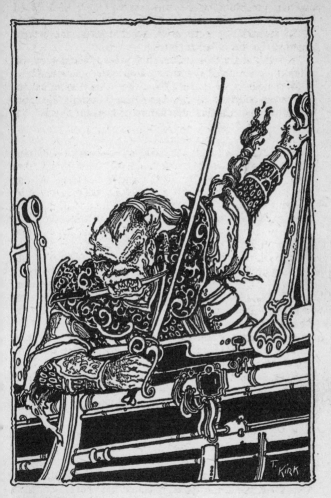

*"A Chuḻik rose into view, his dagger between his teeth."*

I tipped the dead driver out of his reclining seat, and flung him overboard.

Then I stared helplessly at the controls.

"They are smashed, Dray Prescot," said Delia of Delphond. "The airboat cannot be controlled."

The wind thrust us over the city faster and faster. In an instant the mammoth buildings fell away to the dimensions of toy blocks on a nursery floor. They they vanished in moon haze and we were alone, drifting helplessly over the face of the plains beneath the moons of Kregen.

## Chapter Sixteen

# On the Great Plains of Segesthes

If you say to me that, in view of her two suns, Kregen was provided with an inordinate, not to say excessive, number of moons, I can only reply that nature is by nature prolific. That is Kregen. Wild and savage and beautiful, merciless to the incompetent and weak, tolerant of the ambitious and mercenary, positively rewarding to the stouthearted and unscrupulous, Kregen is a planet where the virtues take different forms from those of our Earth.

And, too, as I understand it, Earth's moon and the planet Mars, which is relatively small, were both fashioned from the molten crust of the Earth flung off in primeval days when the solar system was in process of formation. Something like two-thirds of the Earth's crust was thus lost to space, and the floating plates of the Earth's crust, on some of which lie continents, and on some seas, now slip and slide over the molten magma beneath bereft of the building materials that would have given us a greater area of land surface and consequently deeper seas. On Kregen, so I believe, only about a half of the original molten surface was flung off, to form not one moon and a planet but seven moons. It is all astronomically apposite.

Of the nine islands of Kregen not one is lesser in area than Australia. There are, of course, uncounted numbers of smaller islands scattered about, and who, still, can say who or what lives there?

We floated, Delia of the Blue Mountains, and I, Dray Prescot, in our crippled airboat far out onto the Great Plains of the continent of Segesthes.

149

We talked but little. I, because I felt the hurt in this girl against me, the natural feelings of disgust and contempt she must have for me, despite that I worshiped her as no man has worshiped a girl in all Earth or Kregen, for she did not know, must not know, of that selfish passion.

At first she refused my offer of the scarlet cape; but before dawn when the Maiden with Many Faces paled in the sky she accepted, with a shiver. The red sun rose. This was the sun which was called Zim in Zenicce. The green sun was called Genodras. I doubt if any scribe knew the numbers of names there were all over the planet for the suns and the moons of Kregen.

"Lahal, Dray Prescot," said Delia of Delphond when the sun's rim broke free of the horizon.

"Lahal, Delia of the Blue Mountains," I replied. I spoke gravely, and my ugly face must have oppressed her, for she turned away, sharply, and I saw she was sobbing.

"If you look in that black box under the control column," she said after a time, her voice still choked, "you may find a pair of silver boxes. If you can move them apart, just a little, just a fraction—"

I did as she bid, and there were the two silver boxes, almost touching, and I forced them apart with a grunt, and the airboat began gently to descend.

My surprise was genuine. "Why did you not—" I began.

But she turned that gloriously-rounded shoulder on me, and pulled the scarlet cape higher, and so I desisted.

We touched down at last and once more I stood on the prairie where I had spent five eventful years of my life. I was a clansman once again. Except—I had no clan about me.

Our only weapons were my dagger, our hands and our brains.

Soon I had caught a prairie fox, good eating if rolled in mud and roasted to remove the spines, and we drank from a bright clear spring, and sat before the fire, and I stared at the beauty that was Delia's and I found it in my heart to be content.

We had passed over the wide fertile cultivated strip of land that borders this sea—the sea into which the River Nicce flows, the sea men hereabouts call the Sunset Sea, for it is to the western edge of the continent. It reminds me, nowadays, of the sea into which the sun of San

Francisco descends in those fantastic evening displays. We were in the outskirts of the Great Plains proper. Zenicce draws her revenues, and her slaves, the minerals from her mines and the produce from her fields, from all the coast and for far inland. There are settlements of small size all along the coast and for some way inland. I had hopes that if we were lucky we would run across a caravan before we decided to walk back to the city.

I had decided to wait a week. The chances of clansmen finding us were grave; for I could not hope that the Clans of Felschraung and of Longuelm would happen by. Any other clan might well be hostile to us. The girl, then, would be a burden in negotiations. We waited six days before we saw the caravan. During that time I had found a dawning break in the granite barrier that separated Delia and myself. She was beginning to lose that reserve and to be the impulsive, lovely, wayward girl she really was. She would not speak to me of Delphond, or of her family or her history. The only people who might have told me where Delphond was I had not asked—the House of Eward—and the slaves were ignorant of it.

We had made our little camp and Delia helped willingly about the chores. I had fashioned a stout sharpened stave from a sturm tree, and would twirl this about, remembering. Once I had to fight an outraged she-ling. It had crept from a bush and sought to snatch Delia away. The ling lives between the bushes and rocks of the small-prairie, where there are trees and streams, and is as large as a dog of the collie variety; but it has six legs, a long silky coat, and claws it can extend to four inches in length and open a rip in chunkrah-hide. From the pelt, I fashioned Delia a magnificent furred cape. It suited her well. She looked gorgeous and feminine in the furs.

Our first intimation that the caravan was near was not the tinkle of caravan bells, or the thud of calsany pads, or the shouts of the drivers; but the shrill yammer of men in combat and the gong-like notes of steel on steel.

I leaped for the fringe of bushes above our camp, the sharpened stake gripped in my fist. This period with Delia had become very precious to me. Had I deluded myself, or had there been a softening in her attitude to me? Always, she was correct, polite, meek and obliging about the camp in the small matters of domestic chores. When we avoided the agreed taboo subjects we could talk, lazily, for hours on topics ranging from that vexed question as to who was the first creature on Kregen, to the best way of dressing the silky white ling furs, and all manner of delicious speculations in between. Yes, very precious to me was that time beneath the moons of Kregen around our campfire at night. These thoughts rushed through my head as I saw a small caravan under attack by clansmen. Why should I embroil myself? Far better to wait until it was over and the clansmen had taken their booty and such prisoners as would bring a ransom and had ridden off, singing the wild boisterous clan songs. Any interference on my part might well result in an ax-blade through my thick skull, and would certainly destroy this too short sweet period of growing friendship between Delia and myself.

"Look, Dray Prescot," said Delia from where she lay at my side, peering down through the bushes. "Powder blue! Eward—a caravan of the Noble House of Eward."

"I can see," I grunted.

The clansmen were from a clan I did not recognize. When I rode the Great Plains as a clansman, had we met, there would have been bloodshed between us, perhaps; if we lived, the giving and taking of obi. They meant no more to me than the men of Eward. But Delia compressed her lips, and looked at me, and her eyes sparkled dangerously—at least, that is how they appeared to me, for whom, in two worlds, there was no other woman fit to hold the hem of her dress.

"Very well," I said. Lately I had been speaking a very great deal. Naturally taciturn except when a subject excites me, with Delia lately I had, as a newer time would have it, been shooting my mouth off. Having decided, I wasted no time. I stood up, hefted my hunk of timber, and charged down into the fracas.

Men in powder blue were riding their half-voves in furious combat with zorca-mounted clansmen. That gave the men from the city some chance. Rapiers sliced past clumsy guards and pierced brawny chests; axes whirled high and descended to split skulls and spill brains. It was a small raiding party of clansmen—the zorcas told me that— and they must have stumbled on the caravan unexpectedly. I was down and among them before anyone realized a new force had been added to the conflict. I did not utter a sound.

In an instant I had dismounted two clansmen, seized an

ax, swung violently against a group of three who sought to
rip the hangings from a sumptuouslyappointed palanquin.
I had discarded the notion of making a noise as though I
were the forerunner of an army. I was not dressed as a
clansman, nor as a city man—I was dressed as a hunter of
Aphrasöe—and both sides would immediately have seen
through the ruse and all surprise would have been lost.

The ax parted a neck from its trunk, sliced back to
sever a cheek and knock the man from the saddle. The
third man reined up his zorca, its hooves flashing, ready to
swipe down on me, fully extended. I convulsed back and
his blow swept through empty air. The hangings parted and
a head crowned in a wide flat cap poked unsteadily out.
Beyond the man about to attack me again I saw a man in
powder blue sink his rapier into the throat of a clansman,
the blade caught, and he jerked for a moment unavailingly.
To his side a clansman lifted a bow string drawn to his
ear. The next instant would see that iron bird buried in
the man of Eward's back.

I hurled the ax high and hard, in the old clansman's
cunning, and the daggered six inches of bladed steel sank
into the zorca rider's breast. He looked down stupidly and
then fell off.

Then the man facing me was spurring forward and
bringing his ax down. I went in under the sweep of the
blow, avoided the zorca's mouth—with a vove I would
have been already a dead man—and sprang upward and
took him about the waist. We both toppled to the ground.
When I arose and looked alertly about my dagger was
brightly-stained.

"Well done, Jikai!" I heard a croaking voice call.

The zorca riders had had enough. What should have
been a nice leisurely killing and plundering had turned into
a bloodbath. With wild and baffled shrieks they rode off.
We avoided their last Parthian discharges as the bolts
thunked into the ground. If they stood off, we had bows
enough to give them a spirited return to their shooting.

Often these days I am forced to smile when reading the
ill-informed and ignorant usage of words when Earthmen
speak of barbaric weapons. How often one reads that
arrows are "fired" in combat. I have used flint and steel
to fire a musket, and a percussion cap to fire a pistol, and
have fired a high-velocity rifle many and many a time—I
have even used a lighted match wound around a linstock to

fire a thirty-two pounder in the pitching gundeck of a three-decker—but in all this smoke and flame I have never "fired" an arrow. One does not "fire" bow and arrows. Except, perhaps, if you allow that term to those occasions when we clansmen set blazing rags to our shafts and used them to set fire to the wagons and the roofs of our foemen, as we did that wild day in the Pass of Trampled Leaves.

The half-vove rider had freed his rapier. He looked at me with curiosity all over his bronzed, keen face, with the black eyes and the cropped hair beneath the steel cap, and he sized me up as I sized him up. Lithe and strong, he rode well; and I had seen his swordplay—with the last exception of those neck-bones, and they can be lubbers at letting a blade free—and he handled himself superbly well.

He rode over.

He passed me with an intent, anxious look on his face, bent to the palanquin.

"Great-Aunt Shusha! Are you all right?"

The old head in its wide flat hat poked out again. This time more of the old woman appeared, I saw she carried a dinky little dagger in her gloved right hand. Her face was old—old—and lined and pouched with the record of her years; but her eyes were lively enough, bright and malicious on her nephew.

"Don't prattle so, young Varden! Of course I'm all right! You don't think I'd let myself be fretted by a miserable bunch of scallywags like these pesky clansmen, do you?"

She was thrashing about now in attempting to alight, and men ran to let down the steps of the palanquin from its height, slung between two calsanys. She stepped down, small, incredibly vital, dressed in a powder blue gown that had scarlet stitching threaded all over it like sunshine on water.

"Great-Aunt Shusha!" The young man, whom I knew now to be the Prince Varden Wanek of the House of Eward, protested in mock horror and despair. "You mustn't keep tiring yourself."

"Tush and bottlecock! And you haven't even said Lahal to this young man——" She peered up at me with her faded eyes. "Look at him, walking about half-naked, and killing men as easily as I push a needle through a tapestry." She hobbled over to me. "Lahal, young man, and thank you for what you have done. And, it minds me—" She broke off, and Varden leaped from his high saddle and caught her to support her. "The color—the color! It reminds me so vividly ..."

"Lahal, my lady," I said. I made my voice as gentle as I could; but it still came out in the old forbidding growl.

Varden, holding his great aunt, stared at me. His eyes were frank on mine. "Lahal, Jikai," he said. "I own to a fault, it was remiss of me, not to thank you seemly. But my great-aunt—she is aged—"

She tapped his bronzed hand with her gloved finger. "That is enough of that, you young razzle-dazzle, insulting me. I'm no older than I should be."

I knew that on Kregen men and women could look forward, if they were not killed or fell sick, to a life considerably longer than that on Earth, and this old lady, I judged, must be nearer two hundred than one hundred years old.

All this time I had not smiled. "Lahal, Prince Varden Wanek of Eward. I am Dray Prescot."

"Lahal, Dray Prescot."

"You did not see Dray Prescot save your hide, did you, nephew?" She explained how I had thrown my ax to save Varden as the man about to kill me charged. "It was true Jikai," she finished, a trifle breathlessly.

"I had my Hikdar, my lady," I said, holding up the dagger.

She chuckled and coughed. "As I had my little Deldar."

I looked, and, it was true, the dagger was a terchick.

A shout of surprise brought our attention back to the scene around us. Delia of the Blue Mountains walked down the little slope toward us. Clad in the scarlet breech-clout and with the white furs swinging, swinging in time to the sway of her lithe body, her long lissom legs very splendid in the suns' light, she brought a gasp of awe and wonder to the lips of the men. I caught my breath. She was magnificent.

After the introductions were made it only remained for us to ride back to the city with the Eward caravan. It had been to fetch Great-Aunt Shusha from her annual pilgrimage to the hot springs of Benga Deste. Benga, I should hasten to say, is the Kregish word most corresponding to "saint" in English. Beng is the male form and Benga the female, the suffix letter "a" playing a similar part in Kregish as it does in Italian.

I cannot explain why; but when I asked my habitual question of fresh acquaintances on this occasion I felt a taut sense of expectancy. A vague look came over Great-Aunt Shusha's wrinkled face.

"Aphrasöe? The City of the Savanti? It seems I *have* heard of such a place, once; but it is long ago, so long ago and my poor head cannot remember."

## Chapter Seventeen

# A bravo-fighter of Zenicce

Now life took a completely fresh turn for me, Dray Prescot.

If I had missed companionship before, finding that rare commodity at last on Kregen among the tents and wagons of the clansmen with Hap Loder and his like—for Maspero and those, as I thought godlike beings, of Aphrasöe created always in me a breath of awe—I found it once again with Prince Varden and his drinking companions in the House of Eward of the city of Zenicce. And, too, most strangely, I found a compelling sense of friendship, warm and human and very luxurious to me, in the wise companionship of old Great-Aunt Shusha. I owned she might one day recall what she knew of Aphrasöe; but I did not need that hope to make me respect and admire her, and I admit my fondness for her grew almost foolish, if affection can ever be called foolish.

Airboats are rare and precious objects in Segesthes and Wanek sent a party to repair and bring back the one Delia and I had escaped in, regarding it as another trophy wrested from the hated Esztercari. Delia said that she was familiar with airboats, and added that they were not manufactured in her land. That ruled out Havilfar, where I understood the mining was done on which the airboats depended for their lifting force.

I had entered with some spirit into the plans of the House of Eward to take down more than one peg the House of Esztercari. Dressed in the powder blue of Eward I would ruffle it with the other young blades as we strolled through the arcades, patronize the drinking taverns, watch the varied amusements in the Barbary Coast area of Zenicce. I went to the impressive Grand Assembly buildings, and watched as the never-ending debates took place, with men and women walking in and out to leave or resume the seats allotted to their Houses. We even got into one or two bravo-fights, all flurrying cloaks and the clink and rattle of rapier and dagger, and shouting and laughing, and hurried retreat as the crimson-and-emerald of the city wardens was espied, hurrying to break up the fracas.

Once across the canal and within the cincturing walls of our enclave, of course, we were absolutely safe. To break into a House enclave would take an army and although many sporadic raids took place—often, I learned with an amusement so grimly ironic Prince Varden was surprised, to steal a girl—no House felt strong enough alone to challenge another directly. The Esztercari's had by chicanery, murder, corruption and then naked force, ousted the previous House from the enclave and further estates in which they had now settled some hundred and fifty years ago. Some of Great-Aunt Shusha's venomous hatred for the emerald green was explained when I learned she had been a Strombor, a girl of the previous House and recently married into the Ewards's, when her family, her friends, her retainers were killed and scattered. Some had been sold as slaves, some had gone to the clans, some had vanished in their ships over the curve of the world and never returned.

By the twin forces of law and custom all the rights, ranks and privileges of the House of Strombor had passed to the House of Esztercari.

Each House enclave was a city in itself: tasselated pavement, marble, granite and brick walls, domed roofs, colonnades, towers and spires, all the whole gorgeous jumble of splendid architecture enclosed and supported a living entity within the greater entity of the city. The Eward beer was extremely good; Zenicce was famous for its beers, although its lagers, as all are, were weak and dispirited. We young blades would go ruffling a long way to sup a new brew of beer, commenting wisely and with many hiccups on its quality and strength. Zenicce claret, too, is very fine. I looked very kindly upon being a citizen of Zenicce, and of having the undisputed run of the enclave-city of the Ewards with its own canals, avenues and plazas.

There were temples throughout the city, of course, mostly erected to Zim and Genodras; but each House also maintained its own temples and churches to its own personal House deity.

In all this frenzied pleasure-seeking I indulged in at that time I could see, even then, that it was merely a hollow scrabbling at an anodyne. The problem of Delia remained forever with me, and nothing would remove it. I hugged my ache to myself, hating it and yet incapable of cauterizing it. Delia must be returned to her own land; yet to find that land was the difficulty.

We pored over the maps and charts in the library, and I saw with a nostalgic pang how similar and yet how different were the charts of these people. There were portolanos in the great library of the Esztercari's; we could not study those. The globes were so like those of Medieval Europe, the confident coastlines of countries near at hand, the gradual loss of definition as distance threw a pall of ingorance across knowledge until, on the opposite sides of the globes, only the most general outlines of those of the seven continents and nine islands thought to lie there were represented. Aphrasöe was never shown; neither was Delphond.

Looking at the maps, Delia shook her head.

"My country is not shaped like any of these."

I had shared the gems three ways, and Gloag had smiled his wolfish smile, and taken them; but he remained with me as a raffish drinking companion. Delia had pushed the gems back to me across the shining sturmwood table, her face disdainful, her mouth prim.

"I would not take anything from *that* woman."

I kept in a chest those gems, promising myself they were in trust for Delia of the Blue Mountains.

Wanek and his son, Varden, insisted that we regard the captured airboat as our own. Delia took me flying and showed me how to operate the controls, which I found magical and wonderful, and of which I will speak at another time.

During this period I talked long into the night with Great-Aunt Shusha, for she needed little sleep, and I have grown accustomed to doing without all my life. She had witnessed that terrible attack on her House, and had seen the young girls carried off and the men killed. She did not, I noticed, maintain a great retinue of slaves, and, indeed, the Ewards were as humane as they could be, given the circumstances and the nature of the thing, in all their dealings with their slaves.

At last we had fomented our plan and it was time for me to play my part. I had more or less given my word to Varden that I would assist him. The Esztercaris, we had discovered, planned a great rising against the Ewards, and the Reinmans and the Wickens, Houses in alignment with the Ewards. The stroke was audacious; but it could be accomplished, and we must get in our blow first, or we would be lost. Almost inevitably, whichever way the contest went, the city would be up. The stakes at risk were enormous.

From the zorcas and the equipment we had taken on the day I'd helped beat off the clansmen's attack on the caravan I had selected a fine beast and set of equipment. I donned my scarlet breechclout and then over it pulled on a clansman's russet leathers with the fringings. I would say a brief farewell to Delia and then be on my way. It was on this day, strangely enough, that I learned just which girl it was that Prince Varden mooned after, and had told me of during our tavern-times and ruffling strolls through the city. Varden, it seems—and I felt a jolt of incongruous guilt strike through me—had lost his heart to the Princess Natema. He had seen her many times, always with a powerful bodyguard, and his hopeless passion festered in his breast.

"She is promised to another, to that oaf Pracek of Ponthieu. And, anyway, how could our two Houses consent to such an alliance?" I felt very sorry for the prince; for I would have you know he was a true and gallant friend.

"Strange things, have happened, Varden," I told him.

"Aye, Dray Prescot. But none as strange as the chance I shall ever hold Natema in my arms!"

I said: "Does she know?"

He nodded. "I have had word taken to her. She scorns me. She sent back insulting— It is enough that she refuses."

"That is her father's doing. It may not be hers."

"Ha, Dray! You seek to cheer me and mock me more!"

If I told my friend Prince Varden that I had come from

the planet Earth which I now know is four hundred light-years from Kregen under Alpha Scorpii, Antares, and that the strangeness of that must surely outweigh the strangeness that a girl would change her mind, he would have gaped at me. I thought again of Natema, of her willful obstinacy, her complete lack of understanding that others besides herself had any desires that should be fulfilled. Her obstinacy, I knew, was a pliant reed beside the steely obduracy of Delia of the Blue Mountains. Delia had stood at my side as we fought hostile men, Chuliks and wild animals. Delia had even smiled at me over the smoke of our camp fire as we ate the meat from my kill she had cooked. Delia wore the white furs I had stripped from the fresh kill I had made for her in protecting her life.

I noticed that Delia of the Blue Mountains wore those white furs I had given her when she might have had the choice of a hundred furs far more magnificent.

She must do that, I thought in my ignorance, to mock and humiliate me, and I could not blame her for that, seeing to what distress I had brought her, and I feel nowadays the shame of my worthless thoughts; but then I was in agony for Delia of Delphond, knowing, as I thought, that she hated me, despising and scorning me for my clumsiness and high-handed actions toward her.

If Varden had had the same experience with his Natema as I had had, and if he had gone through what I had with Delia, I wondered, very bitterly, how he would regard her then.

Delia was always kind to Varden and, it seemed to me, went out of her way to be pleasant to him. He would be a good match, if the Esztercaris did not slit his throat. But I refused to allow jealousy to foul our friendship.

And so I went that morning in the turn of the year to see Delia and bid her what I hoped would be a brief farewell. She was sitting in a powder blue gown reading an old book, its pages browned and crumbling. On the low seat at her side the white ling furs glowed silkily.

"What!" She started up as I finished telling her. "You're going away! But—but I think—"

"It will not be long, Delia. In any case, I do not think my absence would displease you."

"Dray!" She bit her lip, then thrust the book toward

me, her pink and shining nail, perfectly trimmed, pointing out a smudgy woodcut.

The art of printing varies widely as to quality and technique throughout Kregen; but this was an old book, and the woodcuts messy, the print heavy.

"I believe, Dray, that that is a map of my country."

At once I felt the flare of interest.

"Can we reach it—in an airboat, say?"

"I believe so—but I must compare this with the more modern charts. And, they do not compare. So—"

Then I remembered why I had come to see her, and my promise to Varden. I felt my eyebrows pulling down and my lips thinning, and knew my ugly face wore its ruthlessly forbidding look. "I have promised Varden. I must go."

"But—Dray—"

"I know with what contempt you must regard me, Delia of the Blue Mountains. It was my selfishness that has dragged you through all the dangers you have undergone. I am sorry, truly sorry, and I wish you' were back with your family."

I make it a rule never to apologize—but I would say I was sorry a million times to Delia of the Blue Mountains. She started up from the seat, and her face flushed painfully, her eyes bright and brown and glorious upon me. She grasped the white ling furs convulsively.

"If you think that, Dray Prescot, you had best be gone on your mission." She turned away from me, holding the book in one small hand limply at her side. "And when you are successful and have conquered the Esztercaris, the Princess Natema will be freed from her father's domination. I think perhaps you welcome that."

Delia had seen me in that ridiculous emerald, white, scarlet and golden turban and robes, coming out of Natema's boudoir. She had seen me fighting desperately for the princess' life. She had seen and scarcely understood the drama on that high rooftop of the opal palace, when I had scorned her for the sake of the dagger at her heart, and Natema had had me held over nothingness. What did she think of that? How could I explain? I looked at her and I felt as low as a man has any right to be in his life.

Then I swung away with a clash of my swords—for I wore clansman's gear—and stamped out, seething, furious, sad and empty, all at the same time.

The powder blue of the Ewards escorted me until I was safely well away from the city, and then astride my zorca. With three more in a following string, I galloped headlong out toward the Great Plains and my clansmen.

## Chapter Eighteen

# I feast with my clansmen

Hap Loder was overjoyed to see me.

Truth to tell I had expected some stiffness about this reunion.

But Hap danced about, shouted, thumped me on the back, grabbed my hand and threatened to wring it off, bellowed for wine, hugged me, roaring and hullabalooing so that all the wide camp of the clan came arunning.

They were all there, Rov Kovno, Ark Atvar, Loku, all my faithful clansmen. There was no business to be transacted that night. Immense fires blazed; chunkrah were slaughtered and the meat roasted to its gourmand's delight of tastiness, the flesh perfect, the fat brown and crisp, the juices more heaven-savory than all the sauces of Paris and New York put together.

The girls danced in their veils and silks and furs, their golden bells and chains ringing and tinkling, their white teeth flashing, their eyes ablaze with excitement, their tawny skin painted exotically by the firelight. The wine goblets and wineskins and wine jugs passed and repassed; the fruits of the plains lay heaped in enormous piles on golden platters, the stars shone and no less than six of the seven hurtling moons of Kregen beamed down on our feasting.

Oh, yes, I had come home!

In the morning Hap rolled into my tent declaiming he had a head like the hoof of a zorca, thump, thump, thump across the stone-hard plains during the drought.

I threw him a branch from a paline bush and he began

to chew down the cherry-like berries. They were near-miraculous when it came to hangover time.

The awkwardness I had expected arose from my presumed death. Hap Loder would now be Zorcander, Vovedeer. There was a step in rank between the two, the Vovedeer being the higher; but my clansmen of Felschraung and Longuelm regarded me as a Vovedeer, anyway, even though strictly speaking the name applied to the leader of four or more clans. But Hap was explaining that they were not sure I was dead, that they believed I would return, that he was a Half-Zorcander. I put a hand on his shoulder.

"I want you to be Zorcander of the clans, Hap. If I ask the people to help me in this it is as one of them; not as their Zorcander and commanding them."

He would have been insulted if I'd given him the chance.

"I know you will help, Hap; but I want you to know that I do not order it, and I do not take it for granted. I am truly grateful."

"But you are our Zorcander, Dray Prescot. Always and forever."

"So be it." I told him the plan and then the others came in, my Jiktars, and I was pleased to see Loku among their number. A Jiktar does not necessarily command a thousand men, or the other ranks their multiples of ten; the names are names of ranks and, like the centurions of ancient Rome, command whatever numbers the current military organization demands.

Loud were the shouts of glee when the plan was spread out for inspection. It was childishly simple, as most good plans are, and depended on surprise, stealth and the awesome fighting prowess of the clansmen for success.

Loku jumped up, laughing. "We can find that little thief, Nath. He will help, for he knows the city like a louse knows an armpit."

"Nath?" I said. "Why, Loku, you mean you didn't slit his throat?"

Loku roared with merriment.

"It will be very good," said Rov Kovno with fierce meaning, "to return there with weapons in our hands."

"Bows mainly," I told them, once more their Vovedeer. "And axes. I feel you would be at a disadvantage if you opposed your broadswords to the citizens' rapiers and daggers. The shortswords, though . . ."

There were wise nods. These men well understood the difference in techniques required for fighting astride a vove in the massive cavalry charges of the plains, and those required by close fighting in the streets of a city. They possessed the sheer speed and striking ability to beat down a rapier and dagger man, and I knew, because I had insisted on the art being continued, that they could wield a shortsword in the left hand as they used broadsword or ax in the right; but they would be slow. Maybe it would be best to rely on the techniques they knew, and so I did not suggest that each man carry a main gauche. I did, say, however, tentatively: "Of course, a particularly long broadsword wielded as a two-hander might tickle a rapier man before he got at you." I freely admit I was desperately worried at the thought of my nomadic warriors going up against the sophisticated rapier men of the city.

After all, a rapier is a hefty weapon, quite unlike the small sword with which the French style of fencing is done. Maybe sheer weight and muscle would carry my men through.

"If only you'd consider carrying shields, then your shortswords would be deadly," I began; but their reaction choked the idea off. I sighed. In a clash of cultures the newer usually wins; but then, the clansmen were no babes-in-arms, no novices. I can see now, what I could not see then, the comical reactions of myself to the coming conflict when so much was at stake, that my main concern was with the well-being of as rough and tough and fearsome a bunch of fighting men as I've ever had the good fortune to meet.

Originally I had intended only to spend a single night and day with my clansmen. Already I had seen how effective was the control exercised by Hap Loder, and if a great deal of his success in handling the clans sprang from the tuition he had imbibed as my right-hand man, I took little credit for that, for Hap is a marvelous man at absorbing obi. As a matter of interest he absorbs it like he absorbs the clan wines. He can drink from a flagon with his left hand and swing his razor-sharp ax with his right, in the midst of a battle. I have seen it. I've done it myself, of course; but I doubt if I do it quite with the panache of Hap Loder.

So it was that I spent the next night with my clansmen also, wherein we drank hugely, cheered and clapped the girls as they danced for us—they were never dancing girls, and the man who made that mistake would have a ter-chick in him before he'd finished the last syllable of his mistake—and roared the clan songs to the hurtling moons above.

"Remember," I said, pulling out the suit of powder blue from my saddle bag. "This color is for us. If you see emerald green—stain it crimson with its owner's blood."

"Aye!" they roared. "The sky colors were ever in mortal combat."

At last, and not without a last ten or eleven stirrup-cups pressed on me by my Jiktars and the crowding clansmen, I bade them all farewell and began my ride back to Zenicce. The plan was for me, some miles from the city, to find a caravan and change into my powder blue and thus enter the gates without notice. As a clansman, of course, I would have been an object of deepest suspicion.

The caravan was large and slow and colorful and ablaze with the panoply of Kregen. It had come safely through the prairie limits of the clans, and as well as Chulik guards, there were mercenary clansmen serving in the long lines of pack animals. My powder blue mingled easily with the chiaroscuro of colors.

As well as the indefatigable calsanys, and long strings of the plains asses, there were many pack mastodons. These goliaths could each carry two ton loads, slung a ton each side, and they lolloped along like true ships of the plains. I admired their rolling muscles and massive tread. I hoped that when they reached their destination they would not be slaughtered for their ivory and hides, as often happened, and would once more be able to plod so tirelessly along the untracked pathways of the Great Plains.

The discovery by chance that much of the pack mastodons' burdens consisted of paper—reams and reams of it all beautifully packed—excited my intense curiosity. I recalled the mystery surrounding the manufacture and distribution of paper from Aphrasöe. Coins had, since I had taken up residence in the House of Eward, now formed part of my transactions with life. The Savanti used no form of monetary exchange and the clansmen cared for coins only as booty from plundered caravans, which they might melt down for the metal, or use to barter with the city.

As a slave, there had been no time for me to acquire the small copper coins that often came the way of slaves. Now by the suitable distribution of some silver coins with the face of Wanek finely executed upon one side, and the Kregish symbol for twelve on the other, plus a bottle of the fiendish drink called Dopa, I was able to make an inspection of the paper.

It was fine, smooth-textured from super-calendering, tough with a rag fiber base, and, I judged with a rush of blood to the head, milled in Aphrasöe. Questions elicited the dismaying information that it had come already packed and wrapped in these very bundles, from ships plying into Port Paros, over across the peninsula three hundred miles away, the last port of call before Zenicce. I had heard of Port Paros, a minor seaport serving a hinterland remote enough from Zenicce not to bother that great city. Port Paros was not a great city and did not count; but I wondered why the paper-carrying ships had docked there and not Zenicce. The merchants winked their bright eyes and laid fingers alongside their noses. They would by this mean avoid the iniquitous port taxes levied by the House of Esztercari on foreign ships. Paper, particularly, was ruinously taxed. Alas, no, they had no idea from which land ships had sailed.

Also, they bought the paper at ridiculously low prices and could look forward to a thumping one thousand percent profit in Zenicce.

One unsettling event took place as we made the last few miles to the city. I do not count the cutthroat who tried to stab me that night having seen the silver Eward coins I had disbursed. I rolled away from his blade and took him by the throat and throttled him a little and then broke his blade over his head, lifted him up and kicked his rump with some force, and sent him stumbling, yelling, into the lines of calsanys, which did what they always did when excited all over him. I did not feel inclined to stain my steel on him.

The event was simply the sight of a gorgeous scarlet and golden raptor, floating high in hunting circles above the caravan. That magnificent bird, I felt sure, must come as a sign that the Star Lords were taking a further interest in me. Undoubtedly, they had been instrumental in bringing me to Kregen for the second time, and, I surmised, with a complete faith in my own reasoning, they had not consulted the Savanti as to their action. The Savanti, I often had to remind myself with surprise, the memory of their warm goodness and fellowship so strong upon me, had kicked me out of Paradise. The Star Lords, I reasoned, would regard me as a very suitable tool if they wished to work against the Savanti.

The caravan-master, a lean, chisel-faced black man from the island of Xuntal, an experienced and honest farer of the plains, looked up with me. He dressed in amber-colored gear and cloak, and carried a falchion, and his name was Xoltemb. "Had I a bow with me now," he said in his slow voice, "I would not lift it. I think perhaps I might cut down a man who lifted a bow against that bird."

Questions convinced me he knew nothing of the bird; that only its scarlet magnificence awed him, and the stories told around the camp fires about that serene and lofty apparition.

I paid him the fees he had earned by the protection, as he supposed, his caravan had extended to me and my four zorcas. The fee was reasonable and I had not traveled far with them. He did say, as we saluted and parted: "I would welcome your company if you travel the Great Plains again. I am always in need of a good blade. Remberee."

"I will bear that in mind, Xoltemb," I said, "Remberee."

Prince Varden, and his father Wanek and his mother and Great-Aunt Shusha were most pleased and relieved to see me returned safely.

"The plains are never safe," scolded Shusha. "Every year I must make my pilgrimage to take the hot springs of Benga Deste. I sometimes wonder if I do not fret away all the good they do me on that frightful journey."

"Why," I said, "do you not take an airboat?"

"What?" Her old eyebrows shot up. "Risk my poor old hide on one of those flimsy, scary things!"

Then they all suddenly looked extraordinarily grave. Varden stepped forward and put a hand on my shoulder.

"Dray Prescot," he said—and I knew.

I can remember that moment as vividly as though it were but this morning, when—but never mind now. Then—

then I knew what he was going to say and I believe my heart turned to ice within me.

"Dray Prescot. Delia of the Blue Mountains took your airboat and left us. She did not say she was going, or where. But she is gone."

## Chapter Nineteen

# The Lord of Strombor

The next day I had a little recovered.

Wanek was distressed, and his wife even cried a little until Great-Aunt Shusha shushed her and then drove them all away. Varden stood before me, all his friendship glowing in his face. He lifted his chin.

"Dray Prescot. You may strike me, as you will."

"No," I said. "I am the one to blame. Only me." I could not say how much I raged and scathed myself with deep biting contempt. Delia had been dragged into all these miseries because of me, and I had failed her when she had almost found the answer to her way home. If only I had listened to her! If only I had done as she asked! But my stupid pride had blinded me; I conceived it my duty to stand by my promise freely given to Varden when, I felt sure, by a word he would have freed me from it. I had felt we owed much to the Ewards and I owed them my loyalty. How much more I owed all my loyalty, my life, to Delia of the Blue Mountains!

When a retainer reported that the airboat, the one we had captured from the Esztercari, had been only temporarily repaired and that more work was needed on it to make it really airworthy, I felt no more crosses need be hung upon me. Delia could be adrift over the face of Kregen, a prey to any of the many and various ferocious men and beasts, and half-men, half-beasts, loose upon the planet. She could have fallen from the air in a wild swooping plunge that would end with her body broken and lifeless upon the rocks beneath. She could have drifted out

to sea and be starving and driven to desperation by thirst—
I knew it, I knew it! I do not like, at any time, to recall my
frame of mind in those days.

Great-Aunt Shusha tried in her own guileful ways to
comfort me. She told me of the old days of the Strombors,
and I found some sort of surcease from agony with her.
Many of the girls and some of the young men had gone to
the clans, and most, I gathered, had gone to Felschraung.

"My clan," I said. "Of which they will not let me loose
the reins of leader—of Zorcander and Vovedeer, with
Longuelm."

She nodded, bright-eyed, and I guessed she was turning
over ripe schemes in that devious mind of hers.

"I am an Eward by nuptial vows, and they are a
goodhearted House, and the family of Wanek is very dear
to me. It was Wanek's uncle whom I married. But they
are not Strombors! Only by treachery were we conquered.
I think it is time a new House of Strombor arose in
Zenicce."

"You would be its Head," I said, feeling my affection
for her make me reach out and touch her wrinkled hand.
"If that were so, then I agree. You would make a superb
Head."

"Tush and flabber-mouth!" Then she turned her bird-
bright old eyes up at me, so woebegone and miserable with
worry over Delia. "And if I were, and it were so, I could
delegate, could I not? That would be my right by law and
custom."

"Varden," I said. "He would be a good choice."

"Yes. He would make a fine leader for a House. I am
glad you are friends with my great-nephew. He has need of
friends."

I thought of the great Noble House of Esztercari, and
of a certain enameled porcelain jar of Pandahem style
over-man-height standing in that corridor between the
slave quarters and the noble, and I sighed. Varden and
Natema would make a splendid couple. I had fought for
her there, against the Chulik guards, and Varden would
have done the same.

Varden had something else on his mind.

We were standing in an immense bay window overlooking an interior avenue of the enclave filled with the bustle
of morning market and the cries of street vendors and the
passage of asses and the squawking of birds and the

grunting of vosks, with the slaves purchasing food and clothes and drink and all the busy hustle and bustle of everyday life. Varden tried to open the subject of conversation a number of times, and at last I had to make him speak.

"I know you fought for Natema," he said. "For Delia told me of it. I do not know how to thank you for saving her life."

I spread my hands. If this was all! But he went on.

"Delia told me, and she was angry—how superb she is when she is angry!—that you were in love with Natema." Varden rushed on now, ignoring my sudden start and the glowering look of fury I knew had flashed into my face. "I believe that was the true reason for her leaving us. She knew you did not care for her, that you regarded her as an encumbrance, for she told me all this, Dray, and she was very near to tears. I do not know whether to believe it or not, for from all I have seen I had thought you loved Delia, not Natema."

I managed to blurt out: "Why should my not caring for Delia make her leave, Varden?"

He looked astonished.

"Why, man, she loves you! Surely, you knew that! She showed it in so many ways—the ling furs, the scarlet breechclout, her refusal to take Natema's gems—and the way she looked at you. By Great Zim, you don't mean to say you didn't know!"

How can I say how I felt, then? Everything lost, and now, when it was too late, to be told I had had everything within my grasp and thrown it away!

I rushed from that sunshine-filled bow window and found a dark corner and heard only the stamp of my heart and the crash of blood through my head. Fool! Fool! *Fool*!

They left me alone for three days. Then Great-Aunt Shusha wheedled me into returning to life once more.

For their sake, for pride's sake, for the sake of my bonds of obi-brotherhood with my clansmen, who were riding over the plains toward the city, I paraded a facsimile of normal living. But I was a husk, hollow and dead, within.

Varden told me, with a smile he tried to hide in face of my agony, that Prince Pracek of Ponthieu had contracted with a most brilliant bride-to-be, a princess from the powerful island of Vallia; that the Esztercaris had, however unwillingly, agreed to this match, for it would strengthen their alignment—and this meant, as I saw at once, that Natema was freed. Varden bubbled with the hope that in some fantastic way he would claim her. I told him I was pleased for him. I even ventured out into the public places of Zenicce once more. I had to live now only for my life with the clansmen.

An unpleasant scene developed one day as storm clouds rolled in the from the Sunset Sea over the city. We had gone to the Assembly Hall and, leaving, were met by a crowd of the Esztercaris entering, and with them the purple and ocher of the Ponthieu. In the animated crowds always to be found talking and lobbying in the corridors and halls surrounding the Great Hall there were the silver and black of the Reinmans and the crimson and gold of the Wickens, so we were not alone. ·

Among the Ponthieus walked a tall and burly man clad in a fashion strange to me. He wore a wide-brimmed hat, curled at the edges, and with two strange slots in the brim above his eyes. His clothes were of buff leather, short to his thigh, belted in at the waist so the small skirt flared, and immensely wide across the shoulders. The shoulders were padded and artificially broadened, I saw; but the effect was in no wise incongruous. He wore long black boots reaching over his knees. He wore no single item of jewelry. His face was wind-beaten, bluff, with a fair moustache that curled upward.

"The consul of Vallia," remarked Varden. I knew that in the city there were many consular offices, their functions more mercantile than diplomatic, for the niceties of foreign protocol are not too highly developed on Kregen, and a Noble House would have no hesitation in smashing down a consul's door should they desire for some reason to do so.

The man struck me as a seafaring man, and his manner, quiet, relaxed, reminded me of the calm that deceives before the gale. "They're discussing the bokkertu, I suppose," said Varden gleefully. Vallia was unusual among the land masses of Kregen in that the whole island was under one government. It lay some hundreds of miles away between this continent of Segesthes and the next continent of Loh. Vallia, as a consequence, was extremely powerful, with an invincible fleet. Such an alliance would make the Esztercari-Ponthieu axis so formidable nothing could stand against it. We must strike first, before their plans to attack us matured.

It was on that day, I remember, that for some reason I went to the chest where I had stored the gems I held in trust for Delia. They were gone. Upset, miserable with my own worries, I had not stomach for further upsets and slave beatings, so I did not mention the matter. There was my portion that Delia might have—Delia, wherever she was now!

Now we glowered on the Esztercaris and rapiers were fingered and half-drawn and someone had the sense to send for the city wardens, and no blood was spilled. But the storm clouds above Zenicce were no blacker than our faces, and portended no greater hurricanes and whirlwinds.

A day later Gloag at last reported he had found Nath, the thief, and that Nath would help, for—how I relished the irony—he regarded himself as an obi-brother of the clansmen with whom he had escaped and shared dangers.

The simplicity of the plan was its strength.

No walls girded Zenicce with a ring of granite. Each enclave was a fortress in its own right. An attacking army might swirl along the canals and open avenues; they would swirl as the French cavalry swirled about the British squares at Waterloo—a scene I witnessed for myself. Even the three hundred thousand free people without the Houses maintained their own fortress-like enclaves into which they could retire from their souks and alleys.

Great-Aunt Shusha gave me a surprise. She called me into the long room of her private apartments, and smiled and cackled at me as I gaped at a dozen of her personal retainers. They were clad not in the Eward powder blue but in a glorious, flashing, brilliant scarlet. They looked pleased.

"Strombor!" she said. She spoke the name proudly. "I have made up my mind." She motioned and a slave girl brought forward two sets of scarlet gear for Gloag and myself. "Varden will have need of your strength, Dray Prescot. Will you wear the Strombor scarlet for me, and aid him?"

"I will, Great-Aunt Shusha," I said.

She picked me up sharply. "I am not your great-aunt, Dray Prescot. Never think it."

The affection I believed existed between us made me smother by surprise, for, of course, she was right. I was simply a wandering warrior, a clansman, with no claims to relationship with a great noble of the House of Eward or of Strombor. I took the scarlet gear and nodded.

"I will remember, my Lady."

"Now," she said, her bird-like eyes bright on me. "Go, Dray Prescot. Jikai!"

That evening as the storm clouds roiled and burst above the city the final plans were made. Clad in the gray slave breechclouts and carrying our magnificent scarlet gear and our weapons rolled in bundles, Gloag and I and the men we had chosen, twenty of us, swam the canal toward the island of Esztercari that had once been the island of Strombor. We entered through that low conduit from which Gloag, Delia and I had escaped—it seemed so long ago—and secreted ourselves.

The messenger from Hap Loder had arrived; in the dawn light the clansmen would reach us. Nath would see to that.

We waited, Gloag and my men and I, in the pouring rain, waiting for the first sign of the lumbering wherries easing through the canal water, dimpled with raindrops, from the marble quarries. The waiting was fretting.

So far I have deliberately made no mention of the Kregan system of time-keeping. But that wait was kept in counting the slow passage of the leaden-footed burs. A bur is forty Earth minutes long, and there are forty-eight of them in a Kregan day and night cycle. The discrepancies in the year caused by Kregen's orbit of a binary were smoothed out by the addition or subtraction of burs during the festive seasons, and a similar calculation with regard to days at those times. Each bur contains fifty murs, or minutes. Seconds, although known and used by astronomers and mathematicians, are generally unnecessary in the daily commerce of Kregen. The position of the two suns by day, or any of the seven moons by night, can tell a Kregan the time instantly.

An uproar broke out far above our heads. It was clearly extraordinarily loud for us to hear it, with the rain splashing down into the canal by our ears. I knew what it was. Up there on the bewildering profusion of roofs the powder blue of the Ewards would be spiraling down in their fliers, the men would be leaping out with rapiers aflame. They had not waited! They had gone into the attack early—and I could half-guess that the pride of the Eward House could not stomach waiting for my tough clansmen to strike the first blow. The fliers would be swirling away to bring more fighting men. The emerald green would be surging back, now. There would be death, violent, ugly death, sprawling all over the rooftops and down the stairways of the Esztercari enclave.

And I was waiting here, helpless, in the rain.

By the nearness or the distance of the noise of combat we could tell how went the fray. And soon it was clear the Esztercaris were smashing back the men of Eward. Our allies in the Houses aligned with us and contracted to keep in play the Ponthieu and the others of their enemies. It was between Esztercari and Eward.

The Houses varied in numbers of population and a Great House, whether Noble or Lay, might contain as many as forty thousand persons. Because of the practice of hiring guards, mercenaries, either men or half-men or half-beasts the actual numbers of fighting men available to a House was more than a normal breakdown of population would yield. We had estimated there would be about twenty thousand fighting men against whom we must strike in the Esztercari House. I had told Hap Loder he must leave ten thousand of our clansmen with the tents and wagons and chunkrah. If we failed and disaster overtook us, the clans must have a cadre on which to build afresh. Hap was bringing about ten thousand warriors.

"They have struck too soon," Gloag was saying from where he lay at my side in the rain. "Where are the clansmen?"

Through the veils of rain we stared down the canal until our eyes stung.

Was that a wherry? Shadows moved through the rain as it hissed into the water. Gray shapes, moving vaguely, like pack mastodons, through the mist-veils? The suns were up now and trying to strike through the sodden cloud masses. Was that a harder shape, a long broad shape in the water, with the figures of men like ants poling it along? I stared—and—

"Time!" I said, and stood up and took my sword.

Without a second glance for the first wherry, which now showed its blunt snout over the rippled water, I led my men through the postern to the conduit and, clad in our slave gray, we hurried up the winding stair. The Chulik guards had split, half remained at their posts, the other half had gone to repel the rooftop attack. We cut them down instantly.

Then we flung our shoulders to the windlass and gradually the deadweight of the portcullis over the entrance canal lifted. We strained and struggled and puffed. Through an arrow slit I could look down from the masonry onto the mouth of the canal. The portcullis rose, dripping. And the snout of the wherry ghosted under it, heading into the Esztercari fortress, and in the bows, standing with bow in hand, was Hap Loder. Cheekily, he looked up, and waved.

We left the windlass dogged so that all the remaining wherries Nath had arranged to steal from the marble quarries and which had been packed overnight with clansmen could pass. Then we hurried through ways known to Gloag, down dim corridors and flang-infested crannies, until we reached the slaves' cess-pit door. We flung it open, cutting down the Och guards, let in Hap and my men. Other clansmen led by Rov Kovno branched away at once. Loku would be bringing his men in through the postern conduit opening we had used. Now my clansmen were loose within the fortress of the Esztercari!

Once my men had solid roofs above their heads they dried their hands and then brought out the carefully coiled bowstrings from their waterproof pouches, strung their bows with quick practiced jerks. Their plains-capes were thrown off with the rain slick and shining upon them. The feathers of their arrows bristled from the quivers over their right shoulders, dry and perfect. We went hunting emerald green.

I believe I do not want, at this time, to dwell on the taking of the Esztercari enclave. We killed the enemy, of course; we drove them in a wave of shafts and steel from wall to wall and corner to corner; we linked hands with the exultant ranks of men in powder blue; but we sought to win the victory and not just simply to kill. Where that was necessary we did so, for that is the nature of warfare. But hundreds of emerald green sets of clothing floated in the canals as the mercenaries fled, and gray tunics with the green bands, and we did not pursue. We did not set flame anywhere, for I had told my men that this great House was the home of a noble lady, Shusha of Strombor.

I wore my old scarlet breechclout; and over it the brave scarlet gear of Strombor, as I had promised Shusha. Like my clansmen I did not disdain the wearing of armor, and had strapped on a breast and back, a pauldron over my left shoulder, and arm and wrist bands on my left arm. But my right arm and shoulder were naked, as they had been when I hunted in my Savanti leathers. In the press the blow that kills comes so often unseen, from the blind side, from the back. Armor can save a man's life then. It saved mine.

The final stand was made around the noble quarters in the opal palace.

I raged through that old fighting ground where I had defended Natema, my clan ax biting into skulls and lopping arms. Now it was the nobles of Esztercari we faced. The corridor now presented the same problems. Two by two we fought. I knew everywhere else was in our hands. I leaped forward and hacked down a noble and my ax split along its sturm-wood handle so that the leather thongs sprang spiraling out. Galna, he of the white face and mean eyes, roared hugely and lunged with his glinting rapier. I dodged aside. For a moment, we stood in a cleared space, our men at our backs. There sometimes falls in battle a strange kind of hush as all the combatants pause to take breath and renew their strength before continuing. Such a hush fell now as Galna stalked me. One of my men, it was Loku, shouted and hurled an ax. I took the handle in my fist as it sailed through the air.

Galna smiled toothily. "My rapier will spit you, Dray Prescot, before you can lift that ax."

He was the Champion of Esztercari. A master swordsman.

"I know," I said, wasting breath, and turned, and smashed that gorgeous jar of Pandahem porcelain into a thousand shards. From the wrecked interior of the vase I snatched the mailed man's rapier I had hidden there at the close of that epic fight, and swung up, and stood, facing Galna. I know now my face must have daunted him. But he faced me bravely, his blade a living streak of light in the lanternglow. Our blades crossed. He was very good.

But I live and he is dead, dead and gone these many years.

He fought well and with great cunning; but I took him with a simple developed attack against which his return faltered at the last instant; my dagger twisted his blade and then my brand passed between his ribs and through his lungs and protruded all blood-smeared beyond.

No further resistance was offered as my wolves of the plains surged forward.

We stood in the Great Hall beneath that wonderful ceiling with the lamplight and the torches adding to the crimson and topaz glory of the suns' light through the tall windows. My men crowded about me, their russet clan leathers grim beside the powder blue and, even, beside the Strombor scarlet I wore. Their swords and axes lifted high, in salute.

"Hai, Jikai!" they roared.

A figure in emerald green, lost and drowned now in the surge of newer colors, was flung forward to the foot of the steps of the dais on which we stood. Wanek, Varden, great nobles of Eward, and my Jiktars, crowded the dais. We looked down on that crumpled figure in emerald green, with the rosy limbs and white body, the corn-yellow hair.

The Princess Natema of Esztercari lay there, at our feet.

Someone had loaded her with chains. Her gown was ripped. Her cornflower blue eyes were wild with baffled fury; she could not comprehend what had happened, or, believing, refused.

Prince Varden, at my side, started to rush down the steps.

I held him back.

"Let me go to her, Dray Prescot!"

He lifted his rapier, all bloodied.

"Wait, my friend."

He stared in my face, and what he saw there I do not know; but he hesitated. A man of Eward stepped forward and stripped off the emerald green gown and cast it underfoot so that Natema groveled at our feet, naked. But Natema would never grovel. She stared up, beautiful, disheveled, naked, but prideful and arrogant and demanding.

"I am the Princess Natema, of Esztercari, and this is my House!"

Wanek spoke to her, gravely but with iron resolve that bewildered her. "Not so, girl. You are no longer a princess. For you no longer have a noble House. You own nothing, you are nothing. If you are not slain, hope and pray that some man will take kindly to you, and may buy you. For you have no other hope in all Kregen."

"I—am—a princess!" She forced the words out, gasping, her hands clenched and her vivid scarlet lips curved and passionate. She stared up at us on the dais—and she saw me.

Her cornflower blue eyes clouded and she jerked back in her chains as though I had stepped down and struck her.

"Dray Prescot!" She spoke like a child. She shook her head. At my side Varden jerked like a goaded zorca.

I spoke to the Princess Natema. "Natema. You may be permitted to retain that name; your new master—if you are not slain, as the Lord Wanek has suggested—may give you a new one, like rast or vosk. You have been evil, you have cared nothing for other people; but I cannot find it in my heart to condemn you for what your upbringing made you."

"Dray Prescot!" she whispered again. How different now were the circumstances of our meeting! How changed her fortunes. With my clansmen about me with their weapons raised I looked down on Natema.

"You may live, girl, if you are lucky. Who would want a naked ragbag like you now? For you have nothing but an evil temper and a violent tongue and know nothing of laboring to make a man happy. But, maybe, there is to be found a man who can see something in you, who can find it in his heart to take you in and lift you up and clothe your nakedness and learn to school your tongue and temper. If there is such a man in all Kregen, he needs must love you very greatly to saddle himself with such a burden."

To this day I do not truly know if Natema really loved me or was merely gratifying a lustful whim when she proposed herself to me. But my words struck through to her. She looked bewilderedly upon the pressing men in hostile dress all about her, at the steel of their weapons, at Wanek's iron-masked face of hatred, and then she looked at her own naked body with the heavy chain pressing the white skin—and she screamed.

No longer could I hold back Prince Varden Wanek of Eward.

He cradled her in his arms, smoothing back the lush

yellow hair, calling for smiths to strike off the chains. He was whispering in her ear, and slowly her sobs and wild despair eased and her body relaxed from its rigid grip of hysteria. She looked at him, and, indeed, he was a fine and handsome sight. I saw those ripe red luscious lips curve.

I heard what she said.

She raised those luminous cornflower blue eyes to Varden, who was staring down at her with a foolish, happy, devoted and unbelieving look on his face.

"I think," said the Princess Natema, "that blue will go with my eyes very well."

I almost smiled, then.

A press circled in the hall and I saw a stately palanquin swing and sway in between the towering columns of the main entrance, slowly move toward the dais as the solidly packed masses of men whirlpooled away to give it passage. I also saw a sharp, weasel-faced little man dressed incongruously in clansman's russet and with a long knife stuck through his belt, standing truculently, as though he had conquered everything himself, at the foot of the dais. Beneath the tunic of Nath the thief there were a number of highly suspicious bulges, and I remarked to myself that Shusha would be missing a few choice items when she installed herself in her new home.

"Hai, Nath, Jikai!" I called down to him, and he looked up with his furtive weasel face as proud as though he had stolen all three eyes from the great statue of Hrunchuk in the temple gardens across the forbidden canal.

The palanquin swayed to a halt and scarlet-liveried men helped Great-Aunt Shusha—who was not my great-aunt— up the dais steps. More men provided an ornate throne she must have had carried from some dusty and long-forgotten attic. She sat in it with a thankful gasp after climbing the dais steps. She was so covered with gems that scarcely a square inch was to be seen of her scarlet gown. Her bright eyes fixed on Varden, who had flung a great blue cape about Natema, and who now stood with his bride-to-be to one side.

All the noise of shuffling feet, of laughing, of hugely-excited men, fell silent. There was in the Great Hall of Strombor, that had once been Esztercari, an overwhelming tenseness of feeling, a current of thrilling excitement, a sense that history was being made, here and now, before all our eyes. The light fell from the tall windows and burned upon the colors and the weapons. The torches smoked and their streamers lofted into a high haze in which darting colored motes weaved endlessly. Even the very air smelled differently, tangy, tingling, bracing.

Here was a nodal point of history. Here was where a Noble House vanished, and another took its place, where the rightful House once more claimed its old rewards. The vague thought that I had been brought to Zenicce to encompass just this result flashed upon my mind, to be instantly dispelled.

I knew that Shusha might wish to administer the House of Strombor herself, for her Eward husband and sons and daughters were all dead and she was herself alone—but that she would certainly wish to unite the two Houses in the person of her great-nephew Varden. I felt this to a most happy outcome. She would will him everything, and this friendship between the Houses would be assured. I smiled at Varden where he clasped Natema, and surprised myself at the curve in my lips. His response a little surprised me, for he laughed widely, his eyes alight with merriment as he clasped Natema, and he bowed to me, a stately half-incline. I wondered what he meant.

Shusha of Strombor began to speak.

She was heard out in utter silence.

What she said shook and dumbfounded me, and explained Varden's laugh and bow, for he must have known and approved.

Shusha of Strombor had made me her legitimate heir, given me suzerainty over all the House of Strombor, with all ranks, privileges and dues thereto entailed in law; all the bokkertu—that is to say, the legal work—had been concluded. I was to assume at once the lawful title of Lord Strombor of Strombor. The House of Strombor was mine.

I stood there like a loon, stunned, not believing, thinking myself the victim of some kind of insane practical joke. But my men did not doubt. My wild wolves of the plains lifted their weapons on high and amidst a forest of flashing blades the cheers rang out. "Zorcander! Vovedeer! Strombor!" Among the russet and the powder blue there was now to be seen more color. The black and silver of Reinman, the crimson and gold of Wicken, others of our allies; they crowded in and lifted their weapons and shouted and roared.

"Dray Prescot of Strombor! Hai, Jikai!"

My slave clansmen knew I would not desert them for a soft city life; was I not their Zorcander and was I not sworn in obi-brotherhood with them? So they bellowed with the best. That great and glorious hall rang to the repeated cheers as the swords lifted high.

I looked at Shusha.

Her wizened face and bright eyes reminded me of a wise old squirrel who has stored her nuts and seeds for the winter to come. That stiff slit in my lips twitched again. I smiled at Shusha.

"You cunning—" I said. And as she laughed I went to her and knelt. She put her ring-loaded hand on my shoulder. That hand trembled; but not with age.

"You will do what is right, Dray Prescot. We have talked long into the night and I have seen you in action and I believe I know your heart."

"Strombor will be a mighty House once more," I told her, and I took her other hand in mine. "But, there is one thing—slavery. I will not tolerate slavery whether it be a kitchen drudge or a pearl-strung dancing girl. I will pay wages and the House of Strombor will maintain only free retainers."

"You do not surprise me, Dray Prescot." She pressed my hand. "It will seem a little strange, an old woman like me, going through life without a slave at my beck and call."

I looked at her on her great throne. "My Lady of Strombor," I said, sincerely. "You will never be without a slave at your feet."

"Why, you great big slobber-mouth lap-lollied chunkrah! Get along with you!" But she was pleased. The noise in the Great Hall bellowed and racketed to that wonderful ceiling and I could look down from the dais again.

A man in black and silver was talking to Varden, who had been about to leap up to congratulate me as had the others on the dais, clasping my hand, the first of whom had been Hap Loder. Varden, holding Natema in the crook of his left arm, seized the man by his silver cords, staring into his face. My attention was instantly arrested. Then, the man's laughing having ceased abruptly, he was pushed back by Varden, who came roaring and raging up the dais steps to me. Shusha regarded him with a lift of her old eyebrows. He came straight to me.

I stood up and held out my hand in affection.

"You knew of this, Varden, my friend?"

"Yes, yes—Dray! Hanam of Reinman has just brought news. He was laughing at our good fortune that the Prince Pracek of Ponthieu did not intervene in the fighting, and that they had had no need to cover us in that quarter, for the prince was celebrating his nuptials this day."

"I had heard," I said, surprised at his manner, at once agitated and nervous. "He is marrying a princess of Vallia, is he not?"

"A great match," put in Wanek, with an odd look at the form of Natema shrouded in her blue cloak. I guessed he wished Varden, his son, had made a match that brought with it a whole island under one government, an invincible fleet, and trade contacts firm for ten thousand miles of Kregen. Plus a fleet of airboats hardly seen outside Havilfar.

"A great match, indeed, Dray Prescot!" burst out Prince Varden. "A match such as a Jikai would not suffer to go on! Know, Dray Prescot, that the Prince Pracek is marrying the Princess Delia of Vallia."

## Chapter Twenty

# The Scorpion again

There is little more to tell.

There is little left to say about that time, my second sojourn on the planet Kregen beneath Antares.

I cared nothing for honor, for glory, for the colors of pride, I cared nothing for the bokkertu, for what might have been written down and signed and sealed. My wild clansmen would follow me across the Plains of Mist if needs be. With that marvelous rapier gripped in my fist, with my battle-stained scarlet gear flaming beneath the twin suns, and with my clansmen at my back, I paid a call on the wedding of Prince Pracek and his exotic foreign bride.

The Ponthieu enclave lay just across the canal. There would be trouble there in the future. I might have to raze or capture the whole complex. On that day, so long ago, I and my men roared across in fliers, in skiffs, in the wherries that had ghosted up from the marble quarries with my men packed within. We smashed in with unceremonious power when the place was decked in purple and ocher, and wreaths of flowers hung everywhere and the scents of costly perfumes wafted in the corridors and halls, where slave girls danced in their silks and bangles, where music sounded on every hand. At the head of my men I burst into the Ponthieu Great Hall and a guard of Ochs and Rapas and Chuliks fell away before the ranked menace of our clan bows. Grim and terrible to see, as I know I must have looked by the way the women shrank away from me and the men in their purple and ocher fingered their rapier hilts and would not look at me, I strode down the central aisle. Gloag, Hap Loder, Rov Kovno, Ark Atvar, Loku—and Prince Varden—were with me, but they kept at a distance, silent and watchful.

So sudden, so violent, so vicious had been our descent that nothing could stop us. The first Ponthieu to reach for crossbow or rapier would have died with a dozen arrows feathered in his purple and ocher trappings. I halted before the great dais as the music faltered and died away.

Absolute silence hung in that Great Hall as it had hung in the Great Hall of Strombor—my Great Hall!—only, it seemed, moments ago when Shusha proclaimed my inheritance.

Prince Pracek, with his lopsided face and sallow visage, stood there, his hand gripping his rapier hilt, gorgeously clad in his wedding trappings. Priest were there, shaven-headed, long-bearded, sandaled. Incense smoke coiled, stinking. A crimson and green carpet led to the altar.

And there, standing with lowered head, stood the bride-to-be. Clad all in white, with a white veil concealing her face, she waited quietly and patiently to be united to this twisted man at her side. Bride-to-be! Could I be too late! Then—then I promised, she would be a widow within the second.

Pracek tried to bluster the thing out.

"What is the meaning of this outrage! We have no fight with you—clansmen, a scarlet trapped foe! I know you not!"

"Know, Prince Pracek, that I am the Lord of Strombor!"

"Strombor?" I heard the name taken up and repeated in a buzz of speculation about the great chamber.

But my voice had betrayed me.

The white-crowned head lifted; the veil was torn away.

"Dray Prescot!" cried my Delia of the Blue Mountains.

"Delia!" I shouted, high, in answer.

And then, before them all, I took her in my arms and kissed her as I had kissed her once before in the pool of baptism in far Aphrasöe.

When I released her and she released me she still clung to me and her eyes were shining wonders. She trembled and held onto me and would not let go—and I would not have let her go for all the two worlds of Earth or Kregen.

There was nothing Pracek could do. The papers relating

to the bokkertu were brought and ceremoniously burned. I took Delia of the Blue Mountains—this strange new Delia of Vallia—away with me back to my enclave, to my House of Strombor. Any man who had tried to lift a finger to stop us would have been cut down in an instant.

Laughing, sighing, kissing, we went back to the Great Hall where I showed Delia of Delphond to everyone and announced she was the Queen of Strombor.

There is little left to tell.

How brave she had been! How foolhardy, how noble, how self-sacrificing! Believing I regarded her as an encumbrance, as a hindrance, that I was doing what I was doing out of love for Princess Natema, she vowed to aid me in every way she could. If she could not have me, then she would help me to obtain the woman she thought I wanted, if that would make me happy. I chided her, then, accusing her of weakness and of giving in; but she only said: "Oh, Dray, my dearest! If only you could see your own face at times!"

She had taken Natema's gems, glad now to use them to aid me, and slipped away in the airboat so that I might think she had returned home. Of course, she had known where Vallia was all along. At first she had been reluctant to tell me she was the daughter of the Emperor of Vallia for fear I would demand an immense ransom—which would have been paid, I knew. Then, when she had known she could not live without me—I believe she might have done something brave and foolish immediately after the wedding ceremony with Pracek—she did not tell me because then she thought I would simply see her home and leave, or just send her home, away from me. And she could not bear that.

But when her poor confused thoughts had tangled Natema with me she had gone to her father's consul in Zenicce, that bluff, robust, booted man with the buff gear, using the gems to ease her way in the city and setting the airboat to drift far out over the sea, and told him she wished to be betrothed to Pracek. He had tried to dissuade her, for the match was too far beneath her; but with her own imperious will so different from that of Natema, she had insisted.

I hugged her to me. "Poor foolish Delia of the Blue Mountains! But—I must call you Delia of Vallia now."

She laughed up at me, holding me close.

"No, dearest Dray. I do not think Delia of Vallia an euphonious name and never use it. Delphond is a tiny estate my grandmother willed me. And the Blue Mountains·of Vallia are magnificent! You will.see them, Dray—we will see them together."

"Yes, my Delia of the brown eyes, we will!"

"But I wish to be called Delia of Strombor—for are you not Lord of Strombor?"

"Aye—and you will be Queen of Felschraung and Longeulm, Zorcandera and Vovedeera!"

"Oh, Dray!"

There is not much more to tell.

We were sitting in a room with the sunshine from Zim flooding crimson all about us waiting for Genodras to pour its topaz fires into the room. At the far end were all my friends, laughing and talking and already the bokkertu for our betrothal was taking place. Life had come to be suddenly a precious and golden wonder to me.

As the green sunshine slanted in through the window and mingled with the crimson I saw a scorpion scuttle out from under the table. I had never before seen one on Kregen.

I jumped up, filled with a frenzied, sick loathing, a foreboding, even a knowledge. I remembered my father lying white and helpless as the scorpion scuttled so loathsomely away. I leaped forward and lifted my foot to bring it down squashing on the ugly creature—and I felt a blue tingling of fire limning my eyes and penetrating into my inmost being— I was falling—and Delia was no longer a warm and wonderful presence. I opened my eyes to a harsh and yellow sunshine and I knew I had lost everything.

I was on the coast of Portugal, and Lisbon was not far off and there was some trouble before I, naked and with no explanation of my appearance, could break free and try to make some kind of a life at the beginning of the nineteenth century on Earth.

The scorpion had stung once more.

For hours I would stand, gazing up at the stars, picking out Scorpio. There, four hundred light-years away, on the wild and beautiful and savage planet of Kregen, beneath the crimson and emerald suns of Antares, was all I wanted on any world, denied, it seemed to me, forever.

"I will return!" I shouted, over and over, as I had shouted once before. Would the Savanti hear and take pity on me, return me to Paradise? Would the Star Lords once again pluck me across the interstellar gulf to be used once more as a pawn in their inscrutable plans? I could only hope.

So much—so much—and all lost, all lost.

"I will return," I said fiercely. "I will never give up by Delia of the Blue Mountains, my Delia of Strombor!"

I would return, one day, to Kregen beneath Antares.

I would return.

I would return.

# Dwellers in the Mirage

Beneath the shimmering surface of a lake cradled in the desolate Alaskan mountains, the people of the Shadowed-Land waited for Dwayanu, the warrior hero who will bring back to the world the worship of Khalk'ru, the cruel, destructive octopus god whose appetites must be appeased by human sacrifice.

When Lief Langdon accidentally discovers the people beneath the valley floor, they welcome him as the reincarnation of Dwayanu. Slowly Langdon's personality is possessed by the pride and blood-lust of his warrior ancestor until he is driven by forces beyond his understanding or control to serve the evil power of Khalk'ru.

A classic of science fiction, DWELLERS IN THE MIRAGE weaves a powerful web of fantasy against a background of lost civilisations.

# The Face in the Abyss

A remote valley hidden amid the towering peaks of the Andes and never before visited by civilised man is the scene of A. A. Merritt's classic novel of supernatural fantasy. The valley is inhabited by creatures long forgotten and races pledged to the resurrection of the glorious past.

Into this valley stumbles a young mining engineer, Nicholas Graydon. He defies the commands of the Snake-Mother's invisible but deadly servants and returns to the forbidden valley for the sake of Suarra, whom he loves. But Suarra can not be his until Graydon has persuaded the Snake-Mother to free the land of Yu-Atlanchi from Nimir, the Shadow of Evil. And the way to the Snake-Mother is beset with perils. Such as Lantlu, rider of dinosoaurs; the Lizard men. And, of course, the Dark Lord himself.